JOURNEY TO HAWK'S PEAK
A Montana Gallagher Novel

MK MCCLINTOCK

"The truth will point the way,
and love will be your guiding light."

LARGE PRINT EDITION

Published in the United States of America
Trappers Peak Publishing
Bigfork, Montana

LARGE PRINT EDITION

ISBN-10: 0-9978113-6-6
ISBN-13: 978-0-9978113-6-0

McClintock, MK
Journey to Hawk's Peak; novel/MK McClintock

Cover design by MK McClintock
Cover image © Yuliya Yafimik | Dreamstime

PRINTED IN THE UNITED STATES OF AMERICA

PRAISE FOR
THE MONTANA GALLAGHERS

"The Montana Gallagher Collection is adventurous and romantic with scenes that transport you into the Wild West."
—*InD'Tale Magazine*

"Any reader who loves Westerns, romances, historical fiction or just a great read would love this book, and I am pleased to be able to very highly recommend it. This is the first book I've read by this author, but it certainly won't be the last. Do yourself a favor and give it a chance!"
—*Reader's Favorite* on *Gallagher's Pride*

"MK McClintock has the ability to weave the details into a story that leave the reader enjoying the friendship of the characters. The covers of the books draw you in, but the story and the people keep you there." —*Donna McBroom-Theriot*

For Ethan.
We may live in different worlds, but you'll always have a special place in my heart.

And for my editor, Lorraine.
Even a hurricane couldn't keep you from the book. Thank you for all of your hard work.

AUTHOR'S NOTE

Dearest Reader,

Little did I know that my first published book, *Gallagher's Pride*, would lead to a fifth Montana Gallagher book and yet here we are. Amanda Warren entered the Gallaghers' lives in book three, and I immediately knew she would need a story of her own. Her past held many unanswered questions, and I wanted to learn more about her and how she came to be in Briarwood. Ben Stuart, the ranch foreman at Hawk's Peak, has a bit of his own mysterious past, and the more time I spent with him and Amanda, the clearer their stories became. I hope you enjoy their tender, romantic adventure.

Happy Reading!
-MK

1

Hawk's Peak, Montana Territory
May 1884

A HAWK AND ITS mate soared high above their heads. White clouds tipped with gray created a continuous patchwork in the vast, blue sky, casting shadows over the snow-capped mountains. A cool, spring breeze caressed Amanda's face and whipped her unbound hair over her shoulders. She'd left the house wearing only a shawl, preferring to relish in the warmer air after the long, harsh season.

The winter of '84 had been one of the coldest in Amanda's memory. Although it had been her first in Montana, she was no stranger to the hardships of the western frontier. No matter how settled the land became or how many people from the East ventured in search of the same dreams which brought her parents west, she loved the wildness the land fought to retain.

"I'll never tire of this sight." Not a soul within one hundred miles could miss the grand mountain ranges that crisscrossed the land and protected their valley.

"I won't either." Brenna wore a heavier wool shawl, the edges gathered over her growing belly. Amanda smiled at her friend—one of many she'd made since arriving at Hawk's Peak—and imagined Brenna as a new mother once again.

Brenna and Ethan Gallagher already had one son, Jacob, named after Ethan's father and born in Scotland, Brenna's homeland. The courage to leave behind everything and everyone she knew at Cameron Manor to journey across an ocean and vast continent impressed Amanda. She'd embarked on her own journey when she left home, but it compared nothing to what Brenna must have experienced.

Brenna stopped at a point in the meadow and bent over to pick a few sprigs of wild lupine and add them to the basket she carried over one arm. Calves frolicked in the nearby pastures, another sign that spring had come regardless of winter's efforts to linger. In her lyrical voice with her refined Scottish accent, Brenna said, "When I first stepped foot off the stage, the sheer enormity of what I'd done paled in comparison to the beauty of these mountains. I abhorred the circumstances that forced me to flee, and yet without those trials, I wouldn't be here now. I wouldn't have Ethan or Jacob." She patted her belly and smiled. "Or this one."

"I envy you, Brenna." Amanda continued walking, but it was Brenna who stopped, surprised by the quietly spoken words.

"What a dear thing for you to say, but

there are many who could say the same of you."

Amanda was quick to assure Brenna. "Please, don't think me ungrateful for what I have. I've been blessed many times over in my life. I envy the way you approach life, every day with such hope."

"It got me into trouble often as a child," Brenna said with a smile. "Give yourself time. I often feel as though you've always been a part of our lives, but it wasn't so long ago when you arrived."

Amanda stared across the quiet meadow, fixated on the swaying grass. "Before you met Ethan, did you ever . . ."

"Did I ever what?" Brenna asked. "You may ask me anything, and I'll answer if I can."

"Did you ever wonder if you were strong enough to live the life you always wanted?"

Brenna's soft and understanding smile was immediate. "Oh yes, but then my circumstances were different. I came here for truth, and perhaps even revenge, and I was blind to everything else. Then I met Ethan, and my . . . destiny evolved quickly. Before I realized what I truly wanted, events led me down an unexpected path, for which I'm grateful." Brenna reached for Amanda's hand and squeezed it. "Don't fight your heart too much." Without another word on the subject, Brenna continued walking along the water.

They walked over the low bridge Ethan and his brother had built so the women could easily cross the rushing creek now that Gabriel and his wife lived on the other side. Isabelle and Brenna, both near the end of their pregnancies, visited each other often, and the bridge made the walk easier. Still, Amanda kept a close eye on Brenna as they crossed.

Two new lives would soon be brought into this world, adding to the growing generations of Gallaghers. Isabelle's younger brother, Andrew, and Catie, the young orphan girl who came into their lives at Christmas, were as much a part of this family's legacy as the children born to the three siblings. Hawk's Peak and the Gallagher birthright were safe.

Ethan, Gabriel, and Eliza Gallagher were among the most kind, decent, and honorable people she'd ever met. Without them, there would be no guessing where she might have ended up. When Eliza and her husband Ramsey—also Brenna's brother—found her serving in Millie's saloon, they didn't hesitate to bring her back to the ranch and offer her a job. What a sight she must have been working in the dingy drinking house.

Millie had been kind enough to her and wouldn't allow any of the customers to give Amanda trouble, but just when she would have quit and left Briarwood, the fates had intervened. People like the Gallaghers were rare, at least in Amanda's experience, but it turned out the family surrounded themselves with like-minded and generous individuals.

Amanda once asked Eliza why they brought her home. Eliza had cryptically told her, "Sometimes we cross paths with a person, and we don't always know why we're meant to help them."

The women stopped and watched as two of the ranch hands rode toward one of the corrals where the last of the calves would be branded before they were turned out to pasture. Amanda avoided that part of the ranch once she realized the calves had to be restrained before the hot iron scored the staggered HP brand into their hides. She understood the necessity and knew the ranch hands took great care with the animals. Still, she cringed every time.

Ben Stuart, the ranch foreman, would be working alongside the Gallaghers and other men. Everyone worked on the ranch from sunup to sundown. It was rewarding work, the kind that made a person grateful for the health and strength to wake up each day, earn an honest living, and make a mark on the world. Amanda's mind often filled with thoughts of Ben, ever since he kissed her beside the town Christmas tree as snow gently fell around them. Neither of them had spoken of it since. She avoided him at times when the memory of their single kiss overwhelmed her and when deep and unfamiliar emotions stirred within.

"Amanda?"

She turned to face Brenna. "I'm sorry, you asked me something?"

Brenna smiled and her eyes shined with curiosity. "The last time you drifted off, Ben was nearby."

"Ben is always near. I prefer not to make more of it than it is."

Brenna remained quiet, but Amanda sensed it wasn't because she had nothing to say.

She continued the walk over the green grass toward Isabelle and Gabriel's house with Brenna by her side. They'd brought fresh cookies baked earlier in the morning, and Amanda was eager to arrive at their destination where Isabelle and Andrew would offer a distraction and take their minds off the conversation. In truth, she wanted to avoid Brenna's inquisitive glances.

She thought of Eliza, who had a knack for looking into people's souls and measuring their worth and integrity with her piercing Gallagher-blue eyes. Amanda had long since given up trying to hide her secrets from that particular Gallagher, though it helped that Eliza spent most of her time with the horses in a new stable built farther from the main house and barns. Eliza, like the others, allowed Amanda her privacy, not asking probing questions about how she ended up in Briarwood with little more to her name than a satchel and a few dollars.

Unfortunately, Brenna seemed to have developed a talent of her own for rooting out secrets. With her quiet demeanor and trusting mannerisms, there were times when Amanda wanted to share everything with Brenna. Or Amanda had simply grown weary of hiding. Brenna let the subject of Ben recede and instead repeated the question she asked earlier. "How are the children in town? I know how grateful both Isabelle and Gabriel are that you've filled in at the school."

Amanda relaxed her shoulders and smiled. She spent three days a week in town, helping out the reverend when there was a family in need. She cooked when a mother was ill or in the late stages of confinement, she cared for young children when both parents had to spend time in the fields, and visited with a few of the elderly residents who weren't able to move around without assistance. When it became evident Isabelle would be unable to travel to and from town without great discomfort, Amanda took over teaching duties for a few hours every day when she was in the village.

"They're wonderful, though I suspect they miss Isabelle and are too kind to say so."

"All your time volunteering in town and working here doesn't leave you much time for socializing."

They stopped a few yards away from Isabelle's front door. Amanda held the basket of cookies and a loaf of fresh bread close to her side. "You know I don't mind spending time with the children. I like to keep busy. Besides, I'm no longer one for socializing."

"I heard a rumor the last time I was in town that a young farmer had shown some interest."

Amanda only offered a shrug. "Mr. Patterson. He arrived with two young children a few months ago. He's a nice man and I adore teaching his son and daughter, but I don't share his interest."

Brenna's face softened and her eyes revealed a touch of worry. "It's not my business, but after Christmas I suspected . . . I had hoped, you and Ben . . ."

Amanda turned up her face to the sun and closed her eyes to gain a moment of courage. When she opened them, the pine-covered mountains filled her vision before she faced Brenna. "I've discovered the life I've always dreamed of right here."

Brenna hesitated, though Amanda could see she wanted to say something. "I've seen the way you look at him, or how your interest in a conversation increases when his name is mentioned. You haven't spoken of your life before arriving in Briarwood, and I haven't asked, but is there something stopping you from finding your own happiness?"

"I am happy, Brenna."

"You know what I mean."

Amanda nodded and exhaled, buying herself a little time. "I've feared this moment." She soaked in the sounds of geese flying overhead, the gentle rush of the creek as the water bubbled and flowed over rocks, and the breeze as it carried the fresh scents of pine and spring grass.

"Do you still have family somewhere?"

Again, Amanda nodded. "Some of my mother's family, though they were never close. I haven't seen them since I was a young girl."

"If there's anything we can do to help—"

"Please, no." Amanda gripped Brenna's arm. "If they found me, I'd be dead."

Brenna's rose-leaf complexion lost all color. "In the name of all good . . . Who wants you dead, Amanda?"

2

Iron City, Dakota Territory
September 1883

THANK YOU, MRS. BARNARD. Enjoy this lovely evening."

The slim woman with touches of soft gray around her temples lifted the basket of goods off the counter. "Give my best to your father, dear."

"I will." Amanda held the door open and waited for her last customer of the day to step out onto the boardwalk. The early evening sun cast a warm glow over the quiet town. Off the main trails and roads, Iron City had been Amanda's home since the end of the war. Back then, it had been little more than one narrow road with a few homes and a saloon near the mines.

The saloon had doubled in size since their arrival, thanks to a banker who moved from Rapid City and apparently decided he had big plans for the hardworking people of Iron City.

It was still a one-road town, but it had grown to include two boardinghouses, additional homes built for the miners and a few families searching for life outside the cities, and their general store. Two hundred and fifty souls claimed Iron City as their home, and Amanda Kelly was proud to be among them.

She stood for a few minutes watching the town close down for the night, except for the saloon, which would remain open until well after dark.

Amanda didn't understand what an affluent man from Rapid City wanted with their small and slow-growing town. Most of the townspeople resented his interference, though their dislike hadn't stopped them from going to him for loans in the past. When it became known he'd purchased half a stake in the Iron City Mine after one of the owners died during a train robbery, people looked at him as the man who made their livelihoods possible rather than a nuisance pushing into their lives. Some even welcomed him, believing he'd bring more money and jobs to the area. Irving built a grandiose house on the edge of town, one that looked more like it belonged in a big eastern city like New Orleans or Philadelphia. The house was a constant reminder of his influence and his encroachment.

The Kellys were one of the few families left without an obligation to Baldwin Irving, or his bank, though he made no secret about wanting to partner with Amanda's father and expand the general store into a mercantile, the likes of what one might find in Rapid City. Their small town didn't need such a store, her father had said to Irving, but the banker told

Fergus that he had no true vision for what Iron City could become. Thankfully, Fergus Kelly was a man content and proud with what he'd accomplished.

Leery of those settling the area from the East, the townspeople wanted to live quietly, work hard, and raise their children. Amanda and her family had been welcomed only after the residents realized the Kellys had no desire to change their corner of the Black Hills. Amanda understood the residents' wish to remain far away from the clutches of greed and progress. Had that not been why her own family left Pennsylvania after the war?

When they first settled in Iron City, Amanda was old enough to only remember glimpses of life in Pennsylvania, but she didn't remember any sense of loss when they left. During those first days in Dakota Territory, Amanda saw only the beauty of wide open spaces. To a child of eight years, it was an exciting adventure.

Her father wished to continue farther west into Montana Territory where he'd first dreamed of living. However, her mother's weak heart convinced the Kelly family to stop their trek and settle down. Amanda smiled, thinking of the day they drove their wagons from the badlands into the mountains. Rocks jutted up between pine trees of such a deep green, they appeared almost black under a gray sky.

The Kelly family had chosen well. Along with hard work and the funds they brought with them, they'd built a business and a reputation for fairness and helping others. Still, outside influences attempted to move in and change all they'd worked toward. The people of Iron City were steadfast and resolved to preserve their way of life.

Amanda looked around the town with satisfaction before glancing up at the sign, Kelly's Mercantile, above the store, proud of her father for his vision and determination. She stepped back inside, turned the "open" sign around to "closed," and shut the front door.

She walked through the quiet store with efficient steps to the staircase in the back, and from there made her way to the family living quarters above the shop. A spacious area, it had been home for sixteen years. When her mother passed away in the winter of 1867, Amanda and her father moved out of their small cabin, the painful memories of his wife's loss too much for Fergus to bear.

Amanda reached her father's bedroom, found the door ajar, and peeked inside. His soft snores told her he'd fallen asleep, and when her father slept, it took a great deal to wake him.

Amanda stepped back, closed the door, and returned downstairs to where the kitchen sat off the back of the store. She prepared a bowl of soup for herself and kept the pot on the stove in case her father woke. She'd enjoy her meal while settling the day's accounts.

The minutes spent hunched over the books turned into hours. The lamp she'd lit when the sun ceased to offer light through the windows did little to relieve the strain on her eyes. Amanda leaned forward in the chair, causing the legs to creak. She moved again, but this time no sound. It wasn't her chair. She heard a shuffle of feet on boards, but not from the rooms above. It wasn't her father.

Amanda turned the lamp down until the flame died. She gave herself a few seconds to adjust to the darkness before she walked to the open door. The voices were hushed and frantic, and she knew with absolute certainty that neither was her father. Amanda walked on the toes of her soft, leather boots back to the desk.

With languid motion, she eased open the top drawer of the desk and reached inside. Her fingers gripped the handle of the Colt revolver her father kept near the safe. No bullets. She returned to the door and heard someone stumble. She had left two unopened crates containing mining equipment near the front counter.

"Kelly won't like this. We shouldn't be here."

Amanda braced herself against the wall by the door when one of the men raised his voice. They were closer now.

"I don't care what Kelly likes or doesn't. We have our orders, so find it!" The other man mumbled words Amanda couldn't hear. She held her breath, remaining as quiet and still as possible, until she heard the men leave the store. Her lungs filled once again, and she edged the office door open enough to walk through.

She emptied the money box every night and they kept nothing of great value in the shop, at least nothing that couldn't be replaced. Why then would two men break in, but leave with nothing? The voices, not loud enough to recognize, remained a memory in the air of the quiet store. Amanda searched the front counter and found the papers and items on the shelves below as she'd left them.

Amanda studied every visible corner of the shop, finding nothing out of place except the front door. Moonlight filtered inside, unhindered by the thin curtain Amanda knew she lowered upon closing. She pushed closed the door and reached for the key in the lock only for her eyes to meet those of a man through the window on the door.

"I'm sorry, sir, we've closed for the day. We open again tomorrow morning at eight o'clock."

"I don't mean to be a bother, Miss Kelly, but I think I dropped something on the floor earlier."

Amanda studied the man, yet his face was one she didn't recognize. "Do I know you, sir?"

"Sure, Miss Kelly. It's Barker Pickens. I work for Mr. Irving."

"Yes, of course, Mr. Pickens. Would you mind returning in the morning? I'm dreadfully tired." Amanda knew everyone in Iron City who worked for Mr. Irving. Her fingers began to turn the key in the lock, but the key wouldn't budge. The door eased open and the first thing through was the tip of a blade.

"You're not much of a liar, Miss Kelly." The man followed his knife into the store. "If you and your father want to live, you'll keep your pretty mouth quiet."

Amanda backed up, one step at a time while the once-quiet beats of her heart pounded in earnest. She reached out behind her and felt for the counter. "I don't know who you are and I don't care. If you want money, I can open the safe, just leave us alone and ride out of town."

His lips curled into a nasty smile,

marring what appeared to be an otherwise handsome face. Amanda raised her father's revolver and pointed it at Barker's chest. "Don't come any closer. I'm giving you one more chance to walk out of here before I fire this gun and bring everyone in town running."

"You don't have what it takes to kill a man."

Could he see her fear? He couldn't know the cylinder was empty. "I won't have to kill you to get you to leave." Amanda pulled back the hammer. "I'm only telling you one more time."

Footsteps above shifted Amanda's attention, but it was all Barker needed to close the distance between them. He grabbed the revolver from her hand and pressed the barrel against her side. "Don't move."

"It's empty."

He pulled the trigger and a hollow click followed. The sickening smile returned and he lifted the knife against her throat. "Say nothing and he'll live."

"Amanda? Are you still down here?"

Before Amanda realized what was happening, her father had come downstairs and shouted at the intruder when Barker pulled a gun from his holster. Amanda held no hope that this one was empty. Her father struggled for the gun, and it fired, the sound momentarily forcing Amanda to cover her ears. It was her father whose limp body slid to the board floors.

Barker came toward her with a knife, his gun lying next to her father. He yanked her to her feet by the front of her dress, and his knife skimmed across her shoulder, eliciting a shout from her own lips, a sound which mingled with the ringing caused by the gunfire. In one last desperate effort, Amanda shoved her whole body into Barker's, catching him by surprise. She fell near her father, lifted the blood-soaked gun, and fired. She looked Barker in the eyes before he crumbled to the ground.

Amanda dropped the pistol and rolled over. "No!" She lifted her father's head into her lap. "No, please, no."

3

AMANDA HELD FAST TO her father, ignoring the shouts outside and the sound of the front door opening. A few seconds later, strong hands gripped under her arms and lifted her to her feet.

"Come with me now, Miss Kelly."

She struggled, wondering how long he had stood behind her. "He's gone."

"I know."

Amanda turned and looked into the sympathetic eyes of the town's deputy, Isaac Porter. "He killed him, and I couldn't stop it from happening."

"Come away, Amanda."

The sound of her name on his lips

reminded her of the way her father spoke. "I can't leave him like this, Isaac. I can't."

"We'll take care of him."

She watched him motion to two of the men who stood in the store, waiting to pick up her father's body and two more to remove Barker's. A small crowd had gathered outside on the boardwalk and street, and most of them she knew. Amanda didn't want to look at them or listen to their murmurings. She knew that until the truth was revealed, there would be speculation about who died, how they died, and who was to blame. All the townspeople knew at this point was the sound of gunshots had disrupted their evening and it had happened in Kelly's Mercantile.

Deputy Porter helped her into the store's office and waited until she sat down in the chair behind the desk. When his hand pulled away from her arm, he knelt beside her. "Are you hurt?" He searched her arms. "There's blood here, Amanda."

"I'm fine." She looked at the deputy and wondered why she had turned him down when he had come courting last summer. He was a kind enough man and pleasant to look upon. If ever there had been a problem with a stranger in the store, her father sent for the deputy, not the sheriff. "He had a knife."

"Do you mean Barker?"

Her head shot up and she met Isaac's gaze. "You knew him?"

The deputy nodded. "He worked for Mr. Irving." Isaac took the liberty of cutting a strip of fabric from the hem of Amanda's skirt and used it to staunch the flow of blood from the knife wound. "The doctor will be along soon and he can stitch this up. Someone also sent for the sheriff. He was up at the mine."

"It doesn't hurt," Amanda told him, but winced, holding the makeshift bandage in place when Isaac stood and sat on the edge of the desk.

"What happened?"

She looked up and saw how his empathy battled with his duty to find out the truth, even if she was guilty. "The man—Barker—said he left something behind. I'd never seen him before, and when I asked him to leave and come back tomorrow, he . . . forced his way inside. He had a knife, a gun. I have no idea why he was here or what he wanted." Amanda's sensibilities returned bit by bit. "There were two men in here earlier, maybe ten minutes before Barker showed up."

"Where were you?"

Amanda laid a hand on the desk. "I was in here closing out the books for the day. My father was asleep upstairs."

"The men who were here, they didn't see you?"

Amanda shook her head. "I didn't go out there until I heard them leave the store."

"And your father heard your commotion with Barker?"

"I don't know. He sleeps soundly, but he hasn't been feeling well." Amanda rose, but Isaac placed his hands once more on her arms. She pleaded with him, "I need to see my father."

"They've taken him to the doc's place by now. You should wait until tomorrow after—"

"He's been seen to?" Amanda brushed his hands aside and walked to the office door. With her hand on the knob, she let her forehead fall against the door. "My father was a good man. He didn't deserve this."

She heard Isaac come up behind her, but he didn't touch her again.

"We need to go over all of this again with the sheriff."

Amanda ignored him and stepped away from the door when someone on the other side tried to open it. Doctor Felder, medical bag in hand, ushered her back into a chair. Amanda allowed the doctor to stitch up the wound and bandage it properly, remaining silent. Isaac held further questions until he escorted her to the sheriff's office, where Stratton Cobb spoke with witnesses.

She listened to the sheriff relay a few facts as he knew them, nodding or indicating when she didn't have an answer. The voices mingled one with the next until Amanda's daze wore off and she interrupted the sheriff. "I don't know anything else. The man came into the store, never said what he wanted, threatened us both, and killed my father. I shot him before he could kill me, too! I don't understand what is happening."

Amanda stiffened when the sheriff took the deputy aside, their whispers reaching her from across the small office. She couldn't hear the words, but one voice spoken low and harsh reminded her of the men from earlier, though most men right now sounded suspect to her. The moments around her father's death blurred together. They returned to her side when the sheriff said, "This is most likely a robbery gone wrong. I'm sorry you had to go through this, and I'm even more sorry for your loss."

She nodded once, almost absently, and rose. "I'd like to go home now."

"That's not a good idea, at least not until we clean things up. We can put you up at the hotel, and the doc's wife—"

"No." Amanda calmed herself before an outburst escaped her lips. "I am grateful, but I need to go home."

"Of course." The sheriff stepped aside to let her pass. "Deputy Porter will see you get back."

"Thank you, sheriff." Her eyes met Isaac's for a moment before she exited the office. The deputy kept himself between her and the lingering townsfolk during the short walk back to her family's store.

The familiar jingle of the bell above the door rang when Amanda stepped through. How had she not heard it before when she worked alone in the quiet office? Cold seeped into her skin, though it did not come from the lack of a lit stove or the mid-evening air.

"I'll have some people here in the morning to clean." Deputy Porter cupped her elbow, but Amanda stepped away, wrapping her arms tighter against her body.

"Thank you, but I prefer to do this on my own." She averted her eyes from the blood stain still drying on the wood floor.

"You don't have to do any of this alone, Amanda."

She turned and faced a man who she knew would take her as his wife, offer her protection, and perhaps even a happy home, but how far did the corruption reach? "Please, Isaac. I'd like to be alone right now."

He stepped forward, his booted foot half raised, but thought better of it. "If you need anything, I'll be at the office."

Amanda nodded and watched him leave the store, albeit reluctantly. Her body and mind moved in discord as her legs carried her to the place where her father had fallen, and there she fell to her knees. "You were not meant to die this way. Not now, and not by that monster's hands." She leaned against the edge of the counter and stared into the darkness.

THE JINGLE OF THE bell, a sound she now hated, woke her. Did she forget to lock the door? The dark sky filled with hues of yellow and orange above the trees and craggy rock formations that served as a backdrop for the town, and yet today, she hated those trees, the rocks, the sun. She glanced at the clock on the wall, and tears formed when she saw the small hand on the four. One more hour until she would have awakened to enjoy the solace of the early morning and watch the sunrise. She'd fallen asleep on the floor, but she'd give anything not to remember last night.

"Amanda?"

"I'm here." Her voice sounded as hollow as her heart. With a great deal of effort, Amanda stood up, using the counter to hold her upright. "Doctor, Mrs. Felder. I'm afraid I'm not presentable for company."

The doctor and his wife stood side by side, both focused on Amanda. She could sense their thoughts formulating all manner of condolences while they studied her disheveled appearance and the blood stain by which she'd slept.

"My dear child, why don't you come home with us for a few days?" Mrs. Felder stood half a head shorter than Amanda, but had it not been for the doctor's presence, Amanda would have gladly fallen into the older woman's embrace.

"This is my home, and I'm still needed here, but I thank you for your generosity." Amanda cleared her throat and smoothed back the loose strands of her hair. "Doctor Felder, might you tell young Bobby we'll be closed today? He comes in at six every morning to help ready the store. I'd like to prepare for my father's funeral."

"Of course, but you don't have to make all the preparations alone."

"Thank you for your kindness." Amanda shook out her skirts and walked to the other side of the counter. "Perhaps I could call on you this afternoon for help, Mrs. Felder?"

"Of course you may, my dear. I'll speak with the pastor in a few hours and we'll take care of the details. You leave it to me."

"Thank you," Amanda said in a whisper and watched as they left with much reluctance. Before she could secure the door, another presence appeared in the doorway, the similarity to the previous night's intruder enough to set her hand shaking. Except it wasn't Barker.

She met the sheriff's eyes through the glass and eased the door back open. She wanted only to be left alone. "Sheriff Cobb." Amanda didn't ask him to come inside.

"There will be a few folks coming by in a bit to help . . . clean. They came to me when they heard and asked what they could do to help."

Amanda didn't want their help, didn't want anyone's help, but she knew the townspeople meant well. Her father had been well-liked. "Thank you, sheriff. I appreciate it."

"Miss Kelly, you're no longer in danger with Barker dead. You can rest easy now."

Amanda couldn't imagine anything ever being easy again. "What about the other man?" she asked. "There was another man with Barker in here. I didn't recognize the voice, but . . ." Amanda shook the shock and fog from her memory, the words spoken between the two hushed voices coming back to her, but most of those words had been too muffled to hear.

"Miss Kelly? What about the other man?"

She tilted her head back to look at the sheriff. "He's as guilty as Barker in my mind. The men spoke, but I couldn't hear them clearly enough. Will you please find the other man who did this to us? Promise me, Sheriff Cobb, for I cannot bear he go unpunished."

The sheriff stepped toward Amanda and set a hand on her shoulder. It was a fatherly gesture meant to comfort, but it took all of her strength to remain still and not shrug him away.

"I promise, Amanda."

She nodded and after a moment stepped back. "Will you please spread the word about our being closed today? I know the townspeople will understand."

"They will, and I'll see you're not bothered." The sheriff looked upon her with such kindness, Amanda wondered for a moment if she could trust him.

"Thank you." She waited until he exited the store before turning the key in the lock. She resisted the urge to tear the bell from above the door as she watched him walk away, beneath the scatter of morning stars.

4

FERGUS KELLY WAS LAID to rest next to his wife in a small meadow surrounded by a dense forest of deep-green pine trees. Late summer grass swayed, making time with the music of the wind. If Amanda closed her eyes and lifted her face into the midday sun, she could almost pretend the core of her life had not shattered. Almost.

"My dear?"

Amanda turned her head and looked at Mrs. Felder.

"Why don't you come home with us?"

Amanda shook her head and watched as the townspeople scattered, returning to their wagons and horses, which would take them back to their homes and lives. Amanda could imagine each of them was silently grateful it had not been his or her loved one buried on this day.

The land on which stood had been her father's dream. The small cabin in which they first lived, Amanda as a young girl, still stood facing the jagged rocks rising above the hills and trees. He'd held onto the land, his hope to give it to her upon her marriage—a marriage he would now never see.

Amanda spoke to Mrs. Felder, but her focus remained on the covered grave. "I prefer some time alone right now." She softened her words with a gentle touch to the older woman's arm. "Thank you for your kindness." Amanda repeated the words she'd spoken to others, their meaning somehow now hollow.

Doctor Felder once again guided his wife away, leaving Amanda to her solitude.

TWO DAYS PASSED WHEN Amanda finally opened the store, and only then because she could not expect the people to go without food and supplies. The train was a mining railroad which wound its way into Iron City but also carried provisions for the town. Young Bobby Ross arrived at the store at half past six o'clock, his shock of red hair flattened by a woolen cap.

"Will you be wantin' my help today, Miss Kelly?"

"Yes, of course, Bobby," she said, her voice strong and certain, though she felt neither.

"I'm real sorry about your pa. My folks said to say so, too."

"I appreciate that, and please thank your parents for me." Amanda ushered him around to where she stood behind the counter. "I think you're old enough, and quite responsible. It's time you learned to do more around here. Would that suit you?"

Wide-eyed, Bobby nodded. "Yes, Miss Kelly."

They worked together side by side, tidying the store and going through the same motions she and her father once did before they opened. They continued to work through the morning as customers came into the store, made purchases, or offered condolences. A few, Amanda suspected, wanted to see for themselves the place where the murder occurred. She ignored the glances toward the bloodstained floor and hurried the people along.

The clock on a shelf behind the counter rang in the noon hour, and only seconds later, Baldwin Irving walked into the store with Sheriff Cobb by his side. Bobby glanced at her, uncertain what to do, but she simply smiled and asked him to look after the store for a few minutes.

"Gentlemen, please follow me." Amanda led them into the office. She did not offer them a seat, and she did not take one herself. "What brings you here today?"

Mr. Irving removed his fine hat and smoothed the front of his tailored wool suit. Isaac Porter had been one of many men to show an interest in Amanda since she came of age, and Irving had been among them. Though more than fifteen years her senior, he had been eager in his quest to court her, and for a time she'd been flattered, until she realized his love for money and power surpassed a genuine interest in her. She had kindly turned him down, and in the two years since, he had not rekindled his advances.

"Miss Kelly, I am so sorry for your loss."

"Thank you, Mr. Irving."

He motioned for the sheriff to close the door. Amanda stiffened but allowed him to continue.

"You have a lot of decisions to make, now that you're alone here. I'd like to put your mind at rest and ease some of your burdens."

"What burdens might those be, Mr. Irving?" She watched the sheriff as much as she did the banker. Stratton Cobb said nothing, his expression unreadable.

"This store is a lot of work to run by yourself, and there's your land and the cabin. It's too far from town for you to live out there on your own."

"I live above the store, just as I always have, and the land belonged to my father. I have no intention of parting with either."

"Think on it." Irving replaced his hat. "You could live here in Iron City in leisure, secure for the rest of your life. I am prepared to offer you a fair price for the store and your land. Why not return to Pennsylvania and start over in comfort?"

Amanda walked past the two men and opened the office door. The wretched bell indicated another customer had come or gone. "I'm quite content and plan to continue my father's work in this store, serving the people of Iron City, but I thank you for your concern."

"There's no rush," Irving said as he stepped out of the office. "No rush at all."

Stratton Cobb tipped the edge of his hat to Amanda, and for a flash, his eyes held hers before he followed Irving from the store.

Amanda remained in the office, no longer composed enough to greet people, and she longed for them all to leave. She closed early, asked Bobby to return in the morning, and set off for her father's land— her land now.

"It was never supposed to end this way." Amanda let slip the tears she'd held at bay since driving out of town. Alone now with her parents, two bodies without spirits, she wept for her loneliness, her loss, and the anguish at her father's destructive departure from her.

"When I discover who did this to you,

Father, I swear I will get justice. I don't know yet how, but he will answer for what he's done." She brushed away the tears and pushed back the overwhelming desire to lay upon the graves and sleep until her sorrows no longer weighed down her heart. However, she was not a weak-minded soul, and she would not give into such fragility. Her parents had raised her to be strong, to know her mind, and most importantly, to survive.

She pressed a kiss to her fingers and transferred the gentle touch to each headstone. Amanda could not say goodbye. She climbed into the wagon's seat, adjusting the skirt of her long, calico dress. The sun teased of a beautiful setting, and though Amanda hesitated once more to leave, the last glimpse at her parents' graves gave her the courage to face her demons.

The sunset on the horizon appeared far too bright, much too concentrated and close to the ground. A panic welled inside as Amanda urged the horse faster toward town. She smelled the smoke at the same time she saw the gray and white billows rising above the buildings on one side of the street.

She did not doubt the source of the fire, and two alarming thoughts raced through her mind: Was the store empty, and could they clear the surrounding buildings before the barrels of gunpowder inside ignited?

5

A JUMBLE OF CONCERNED shouts and cries filled the air as the townspeople rushed to extinguish the fire. Water sloshed over the edges of pails as they were carried from the well in the center of town to the burning building.

Momentarily frozen, Amanda stared as the flames danced and mocked her even as they consumed her father's store. The cry of a woman broke through, and Amanda shouted for a boy running past, one too young to do much but get in the way, to take her horse and wagon to the livery. His older sister grabbed the reins instead and together they ran toward the opposite side of the small town.

Amanda picked up a discarded bucket, refilled it, and rushed to join the others.

The heat seemed to bake through her clothes, scorching her skin. The smoke, darker in some places, heaved before it retreated on itself.

"Bobby!" The scream wrenched through Amanda. The boy's mother ran toward her. "I don't know where Bobby is!"

Amanda had never wanted to know what it might be like for her heart to stop, but in that second, she could imagine. "He was supposed to leave the store an hour ago."

"He never came home!"

A hand clamped down on Amanda's shoulder. She dropped the bucket in her haste to turn around.

"Amanda! Where have you been?"

"Isaac, listen to me. Bobby is missing. He could have been inside. We have to find him!"

"We need to get everyone away, Amanda. The fire is too far gone."

"We have to find Bobby! Wait—oh, Isaac, please!" She stepped closer, grabbed his arm. "There are two barrels of gunpowder in the storeroom."

"God Almighty," Isaac whispered, and pushed her away. He raised his gun into air and fired, the sudden noise startling everyone around the fire. "Get back, all of you! It's going to blow!"

The rest happened too quickly for Amanda to recall each step that took her farther and farther from the burning building. She didn't see the explosion but heard the deafening sound and immediate echo. The heavy body covering hers prevented even the slightest movement.

SOOT-COVERED FACES SAT atop weary bodies as men, women, and children moved closer to the destruction. Mercifully, the only structure to fall victim to the fire was Kelly's Mercantile. A small fire had started and was put out at the telegraph office, the closest building to the store.

The rest of the men had come down from the mines and together the town had put out the remaining flames. Heat and smoke continued to rise from the charred remnants. Isaac stood beside her looking upon the damage when Sheriff Cobb and Baldwin Irving arrived in a wagon pulled by two horses that appeared to have been run too hard.

"We heard the explosion, then saw the smoke." Cobb tossed the reins to Irving and jumped down from the wagon. "Was anyone hurt?"

Amanda wouldn't look at him. "We can't find Bobby Ross."

"And where were you, Miss Kelly?" Irving asked, having climbed down from the wagon. His dark suit appeared to carry a little dust from the drive into town, and even those specks he now brushed away.

"Mr. Irving, let me handle this," Cobb said.

The words she wanted to say were stuck behind anger and overwhelming sadness. It was Isaac who came to Amanda's defense, for which she was grateful.

"Miss Kelly came back to town after the fire was started, Sheriff Cobb. Besides, she wouldn't do something like this and you know it."

"No, I don't know that and neither do you," Irving said. "A young boy may be dead and someone has to answer for it."

Amanda faced him, no longer able to contain herself. "What right do you have to accuse me?"

Irving ignored her. "Sheriff Cobb, I demand you take her into custody until we're able to ascertain what has happened."

Amanda scoffed, not believing the sheriff would arrest her on the banker's say-so. She was wrong.

"I'm sorry, Miss Kelly, but it will only be for a day or two while we conduct an investigation. You understand?"

Isaac stepped in front of her. "Now, sheriff, I'm telling you, she came into town after the fire started. Besides, we don't know yet if Bobby was inside. He likes to go hunt. Could be he's lost."

The sheriff moved around Isaac. "It's well known you've had your sights on Miss Kelly, Isaac. You know I can't take your word for it when I believe you may simply be protecting her."

"Isaac." Amanda placed a soft hand on his arm. "It's all right. Please, just find Bobby."

A STRONG HAND OVER her mouth woke Amanda from a listless sleep. She turned over but whoever silenced her kept a firm grip on her body. Moonlight streamed in through one of the two small windows in the jail cell. In the darkness, she saw a man's figure. The haze lifted from her mind as recognition set in.

He removed his hand and pressed a finger to his lips. She nodded to tell him she understood she must remain quiet. The door to the cell was open and they walked through. No one sat at the desk or stood watch.

Amanda stopped him, stepped close to whisper, "Where is the man who was here?"

Isaac shook his head and led her from the sheriff's office. He pressed her against the side of the building as he hurried her around the corner. The office backed up to a slight rise and a thick forest. Shadows obscured their progress into the trees, but she stopped when she heard a soft nicker.

Her father's piebald mare drew her attention. Isaac didn't give her a chance to ask questions. He led her to the horse, already saddled, and pushed her up and onto the animal's back.

"Isaac, wait. It will be better for me to stay and fight this."

"No, Amanda, it won't. Irving will find a way to blame this on you, and Sheriff Cobb will have to go along with it."

"But why?"

Guilt flashed for a second in his eyes, but it was long enough for Amanda to realize that Isaac Porter, the man she'd called friend, was in deeper than she realized.

"No, Isaac, not you."

He ignored her plea for answers.

"There's a bag with some food, enough money to make a new start, and some clothes I borrowed from my sister. You're about the same size."

Amanda didn't have words enough to express either her dismay or her gratitude, so she said nothing, even as her mind screamed for—no, demanded—answers. He would not be able to justify himself if he truly had been involved, no matter how indirectly, with her father's death.

She studied his face, his expression racked with remorse, testifying to his culpability. But in what, and how deep into the town did the deception spread? Amanda wouldn't have her explanations this night. Given the choice of running or facing whatever they had planned for her, Fergus Kelly would have wanted her to live to clear her name and fight for what was hers.

Amanda sensed Isaac's watching her as she guided the horse along the edge of the forest and rode out of town with nothing except nature's silence as her companion.

6

EXCUSE ME?"

The woman wore her hair in a tight bun beneath a bonnet that wouldn't offer her much protection as the weather turned. She held a toddler on her hip and a curious look in her eyes.

"May I help you, miss?"

"I hope so. Are these wagons headed west?"

The woman nodded and shifted the boy from one hip to the other. "They are."

Amanda remained still as the woman gave her a careful study. She didn't blame her for the cautious appraisal, not when Amanda stood before her alone, travel-weary, and covered in trail dust and mud.

"I wonder if I might join you for a few days. I can pay."

"Are you running from the law?"

Amanda choked back a shaky laugh. "No, ma'am. My father's died and I have no one else, so I set out on my own."

"You look strong enough. Can you cook?"

"I can."

The woman set the boy on the ground when he squirmed in her arms. "The others will have to agree. The name's Louisa Baxter."

Amanda released a slow breath and gave a response as close to the truth as she could. "Amanda Warren."

Amanda didn't have long to wait for her answer since one of the women in the group was seven months pregnant and another on the weaker side. They were happy to have the extra help with cooking and the children.

The next morning, three prairie

schooners set out of Lead, South Dakota. It cost her half of the money Isaac had given her, but she couldn't go into a town where someone might be looking for someone with her description. She wouldn't doubt Cobb had already sent telegrams to nearby towns, and she couldn't continue to venture any farther alone. When it came time to stop running, she'd need to find work. Until then, she had to put as much distance between her and Iron City as possible.

7

Hawk's Peak, Montana Territory
May 1884

THE BASKET OF SPRING flowers swung lightly at Amanda's side as she and Brenna walked back to the house after their visit with Isabelle. The inviting veranda welcomed them to sit and enjoy more time outside while Brenna rested in the new rocking chair Ethan had built last month.

"Now you know why I left home." Amanda settled into one of the other chairs and lowered the basket to the boards.

Brenna rocked back and forth in an unhurried motion, and if Amanda read her friend correctly, Brenna didn't appear in the least bothered by what she had revealed.

"Are you certain it was this man, Baldwin Irving, who destroyed your store and was somehow involved with your father's death?"

Amanda lifted a single stem of lupine from the basket and brushed it over her palm. "No, I'm not certain, in that I don't have proof. At some point, I suppose I decided they didn't care enough to come after me or didn't suspect I knew the truth. I'm happy here, and I don't want to leave."

"There's no reason you have to leave— ever." Brenna held her hand open and waited for Amanda to accept it.

"I'm technically wanted by the law, Brenna, however unjust the motives."

"You are part of this family, and I promise you, whatever may happen in life—good or bad—we'll be here for you. Besides, it doesn't sound as though this sheriff has any business calling himself a lawman."

Their hands parted, but Amanda could still feel the warmth and compassion of Brenna's touch. Only her mother and father had been able to comfort her with such a simple connection. No, she corrected herself, they weren't. She thought of Ben and the kiss they had shared at Christmas, but there was nothing uncomplicated about the kiss. Amanda convinced herself that her past prevented her from opening her heart to the possibility of a future with Ben, but it was fear. She knew what Ben wanted because his hopes were a reflection of her own.

"I know I'm safe here, and yet I can't allow myself to move forward until I'm convinced they won't show up one day and . . ." Would they kill her? Is there a warrant for Amanda Kelly's arrest? She couldn't be positive. Why then did she hold such a tremendous fear within her heart?

"Is this why you've kept Ben at a distance?"

Amanda turned away from the horses in the corral and looked at Brenna. "You've noticed."

Brenna smile was sympathetic. "We've all noticed, most especially Ben, though I daresay he'll will wait for you until the end of his days."

"He doesn't even know my real name." Amanda rose and walked to the railing.

"It's your choice who you tell, but the family deserves to know. They can't help if you keep this secret from them." Brenna maneuvered herself out of the rocking chair and joined Amanda at the railing.

"I'm grateful, of course, but it's not your duty—or responsibility—to protect me. You've given me a home and a second chance for a good life. I don't want to mess up this opportunity, but what worries me more is that I could endanger any of you."

Brenna smiled, turned, and leaned with

her back against the rail. "Haven't you learned by now, the Gallaghers protect their own."

Amanda turned at the sound of laughter drifting through one of the open windows. Catie and Jacob's joy filled the air, a reminder of the life she could continue to have if she stopped running from her past, and most especially from fear.

"I think I'll join them." Brenna walked toward the front door, then turned back to face Amanda. "You choose the time to tell the family, but if anyone deserves the truth, it's Ben, and sooner would be best. Otherwise, Amanda, you should set him free."

8

AMANDA AVOIDED BEN FOR two more days and kept any conversations with Brenna to everyday topics regarding family and the ranch. It helped that she spent most of those two days in town helping the new teacher at the school, a matronly widow from Billings who had arrived the week prior and adored children. Mrs. Carver had retired a dozen years earlier. However, after her husband passed away, she decided to fill her days doing what she loved—teaching young minds.

The children had taken to Mrs. Carver immediately, which was no surprise to Amanda. She was a woman brimming with stories of life in the East, the war between the North and South, and of her adventures as a pioneer on the journey west, a not-so-terrifying encounter with Indians, and settling in Montana fifteen years ago. Amanda's own journey seemed tame by comparison. Except, Amanda knew that Mrs. Carver didn't have a wanted poster on her.

The post as schoolteacher had been offered to Amanda, and though she lacked the experience of a formal teacher, she had considered the position. It was only when she saw the difficulty of Brenna's pregnancy and learned Isabelle would have to be abed most days, that she needed—and wanted—to be at the ranch.

"Amanda, dear?"

She shook overcrowding thoughts away and faced the teacher. "I'm sorry, Mrs. Carver, I didn't hear you."

"Please, when the children aren't around, I do hope you'll call me Flora."

"Of course, Flora." Amanda dropped the rag she'd used to clean the blackboard into the laundry bucket.

"You have a good deal too much on your mind for someone so young." Flora stacked the books she'd used in today's class back on the narrow bookshelf behind her desk. "Would you like to talk about it?"

"I have a decision to make, a difficult one."

"Will your decision have consequences for you or for others?"

"Possibly both." She lowered herself onto one of the benches behind a student's desk, her mind and body weary from the weight of the secret. "I have a story of sorts, and I've shared it with only one person, but there's someone in particular who deserves to be told."

"And you're worried if you tell this person, he or she won't understand?"

Amanda thought of Ben and imagined what he might say or do. "He'll understand."

"I see." Flora sat down in the bench across from Amanda. "I was well into my twenties when my William asked for my hand. News of the war breaking out reached us, and he told me he'd be leaving to join the northern cause. I refused to marry him."

Flora's voice softened, and to Amanda it appeared Flora had drifted with her thoughts to another time.

"Four long years I waited and regretted. By the grace of God he came back to me, but I almost lost my chance at real love." Flora rested her arms on the desk and leaned forward as though her next words were the most important. "Whatever your secret, learn from an old woman's mistakes and don't risk not telling this young man. No matter how he reacts. If he means something to you, a good, solid foundation is what you need, and nothing builds that better than honesty."

"And love?" Amanda asked, her lips turning into a soft smile.

"And love." Flora stood and patted Amanda's cheek in a motherly gesture. "It's time for you to go home now and decide what you'll do next."

Amanda returned to the Gallaghers' cottage the family used when they preferred to remain in town overnight, especially during the winter months. Two or three nights per week, Amanda made use of the cozy dwelling, and considered herself blessed to be counted among their family. They told her often, and yet there were times when she wondered if a true family member would keep secrets like the one she held.

It was time for her to go back to the ranch—and Ben—and as Flora said, decide what to do next. Amanda had already made the decision. In truth, she'd made it the moment she resolved to share her story with Brenna. The choice she had to make next was whether to stay and possibly endanger the family or move on and confront what may be following her.

In the afternoon, Amanda closed up the cottage and saddled the mare. With her hand on the pommel and one foot in the stirrup, she pulled herself halfway onto the horse when a wagon drove up behind her. She stumbled back when she saw who sat on the driver's bench.

Strong arms lifted her off the dusty ground.

"Are you all right?"

Amanda looked from Ben to the wagon and wondered how he reached her so fast. "The only injury is to my pride. Thank you."

"You're welcome." His hands lingered for a second on her arms before he stepped back. "Except I have a feeling I'm the reason you fell. I'm not sure if that's a good or bad thing," he said with a slight grin.

She wondered how he became more

handsome every time she saw him.

"I was just surprised and didn't have a good foothold in the stirrup." Amanda shook out her skirts to no avail. The dirt would remain until she could scrub it away. "I didn't know anyone from the ranch was coming into town today."

"We've been expecting a shipment of supplies for the bunkhouse expansion."

Ben removed his hat to reveal thick, blond hair in need of a trim, though Amanda liked the way it fell over his brow after he ran a hand through it.

"I thought I'd offer you a ride back to the ranch . . . if you want the company."

Amanda didn't really want a traveling companion until he'd arrived. She'd grown accustomed to longer hours in the saddle, providing her time to think, since her arrival at Hawk's Peak. Today, she needed to think, and though she spent most of her time at the ranch, she enjoyed her rides to and from town. Ben's warm, brown eyes brightened beneath the glare of waning sunshine, and Amanda realized she wouldn't have a better opportunity to speak with him.

"I would enjoy the company. Thank you." She waited for him to secure the horse to the back of the wagon and accepted his help onto the bench. They set out on the open road leading from the small town of Briarwood to Hawk's Peak ranch. The main road led to nowhere else except the ranch, something which had brought Amanda great comfort. If someone planned to surprise her, he or she wouldn't have an easy time of it, either passing through Briarwood or riding onto Gallagher land and risk being seen.

More than six months had passed since her arrival, yet she still allowed fear to creep into her thoughts. Telling Brenna had been a first step, a test to convince herself she could share her story without fear. Now it was time for the next step.

"Is everything all right, Amanda?"

She sat close enough to Ben for their shoulders to brush as the wagon rolled along the dirt road. His eyes sought hers and she allowed them to draw her in for a few seconds before she faced forward. "Are we friends?"

Ben stiffened beside her; a slight shift to his body was all it took for her to feel the change. He kept his voice even and light when he replied, "Of course we are."

Amanda inhaled, mustered much-needed courage, and exhaled deeply. "There's something I'd like to tell you." She turned her head after a few seconds of silence to see if he watched her or the road. A comforting thrill coursed through her when she saw the intensity in his eyes. Did he know? she wondered. He somehow read her so well—too well at times—and yet he never pushed or demanded she tell him anything.

"There's no need if whatever you have

to say makes you so nervous." Ben continued to look at her in between quick glances forward. The sure-footed horses apparently knew their way home. "If you take one more deep breath to calm your nerves, you'll end up with half of the road dust in your lungs."

It was said in a kind, lighthearted tone, but Ben didn't smile. Amanda began to take another deep breath and stopped herself, almost choking on air. "I am out of sorts, but it's not . . . it's because . . . oh, for goodness sake."

"Amanda."

Her name came whisper-soft from his lips. A shadow of Ben's easy smile returned. "You don't have to, but please know you can tell me anything." He pulled the horses to a gentle stop and faced her. "Anything."

9

Tongue River Valley, Montana Territory
September 9, 1883

HE TIPPED HIS HAT and smiled at her every time he rode past on his tall, bay gelding. One of two unmarried guides in the wagon train, Reed Slater was a man of strong bearing. Although not much taller than Amanda, he possessed a lean build and wide shoulders.

His strength became evident after she watched him working around the camp night after night. He was the first of the men to help out when an extra pair of hands was needed or a child wanted to be entertained by stories of the western plains. During one such storytelling evening, Amanda stopped to listen alongside the children, the youngest girl on her lap. It was a tale of the northern Cheyenne who lived in the same valley through which they now traveled.

One of the young boys raised his hand and asked Reed, "Will we see any Cheyenne?"

"We just might."

"Will they hurt us?" asked a girl named Molly.

"Nah. We'll keep you safe. Most of them are real friendly if you're friendly to them."

The story continued with a few more questions and giggles. The tension eased from Amanda's shoulders as she studied the faces around the campfire. She had found a place to hide, and if only for a short time, to feel safe.

The small band of three wagons had joined with a larger group, and the wagon master—a Jameson Cooke—had readily welcomed them. Amanda remained uneasy until she heard Cooke tell another man in their smaller wagon train that they'd been laid up for a week while one of the women gave birth. Amanda's ease came knowing it was unlikely they'd heard about a woman matching her description who had escaped from jail.

Reed Slater was the type of man she wouldn't have given much thought to had he walked into the mercantile back in Iron City, though he made himself known to her when her smaller party joined up with his group. Handsome enough, but she knew her father always had higher aspirations for her. For a time, when Baldwin Irving had shown an interest, Amanda feared her father might approve of such a match. Thankfully, she needn't have worried.

Fergus had disliked Irving, and his persistence to buy out, or even partner with, her father had become an annoyance. When the banker offered a ridiculous amount for the land upon which Fergus had built their first cabin, her father refused, and told the man that his land, his store, and his daughter were not for sale.

Relations had been strained between the banker and the general store owner for a few months after their conversation, but afterward it was as though the animosity— or at least Irving's recollection of it— ceased to have happened.

Amanda would never forget what her father had told her the night after Irving vocalized his desire to court her. "Amanda, my girl," he had said. "Give your heart wisely, for love is the only light that shines brightly enough to guide you through the worst of life's storms." She knew it must have been the same way between her parents, for only a man who had truly loved a woman would speak such poetic words and know their truth.

She didn't know if she'd ever feel so

strongly about someone, but she held those words close to her heart, a shield against choosing wrong, and a guide to know the truth when she came face-to-face with it.

Out here, by the glow of the campfire and beneath the black sky dotted with the brilliance of heaven's light, Amanda allowed herself a moment of hope.

"Glad to see you joined in story time tonight."

How did Amanda not hear him approach? She tilted her face back to admire the vast sky sprinkled with bright stars. That's why. She and her father used to enjoy watching the stars on clear nights. He would tell her that one day, if they waited with enough patience, a star would soar through the sky and grant her a wish.

Amanda had yet to see a falling star or have a wish granted. "It's a nice way to end a long day." The children were now abed, and the soft murmur of voices from around the campfires dwindled. Here on the edge of the camp beside one of the supply wagons, Amanda sought for a few moments of solitude. "I should turn in."

Reed shifted his body, a subtle move accompanied by an easy smile. "It's too pretty of a night to go to sleep now." He swept his hat off and gestured toward the night sky. "Have you ever seen anything so beautiful?"

Amanda looked back up. "It is lovely."

"Makes a person wonder how God thought to make someone like me after he made all of that." Reed replaced his hat and widened his grin. "Stay and enjoy it a bit longer with me."

Her solitude now a memory, the cool, night air ruffled the edges of her shawl, and her weary mind desired only rest. "I really should get to sleep. It's been a grueling day and we have to be ready to leave early." Amanda said all of this with an easiness to her voice which vanished when Reed gripped her arm. Her eyes remained fixed to his, a silent warning. When he didn't loosen his grip, she said, "You've overstepped, Mr. Slater."

"I see the way you look at me, Amanda." He reached out and brushed aside a loose strand of her hair. "I've never known anyone so beautiful."

"Reed, please. I'm tired and I know you must be as well." She pulled her arm away. She wouldn't be surprised if he'd left her with bruises. "Why don't we forget this happened and I'll see you in the morning."

This time Reed's arm snaked around her waist. "I'm not tired."

"Well, I am. But not too tired to scream." She refused to show any fear. Voices reached them from the other side of the supply wagon. The other guide slept on a bedroll on this side of the camp. She was safe enough, unless he managed to drag her away from the camp, and Reed must have realized it. It wouldn't take much of a shout to draw attention their way.

His strong hand covered her mouth, his other held her arms against her body. For a minute, Amanda believed he might carry her into the darkness. Against her ear his voice spoke in a low whisper. "You know what I can do to you?"

She didn't think he expected a response, but she nodded anyway.

"Good. You keep quiet now, I'll walk away easy like, and we'll do what you said and forget all about this."

"You out there, Reed?"

Amanda struggled against him and he released her. Placing a finger over his lips, he walked away. "I'm here, Bob. Everyone tucked in for the night?" His voice faded as he moved farther away.

Amanda braced her shaky arms against the wagon and inhaled the cold night air in an effort to clear her thoughts, and along with it, the urge to run to the wagon master and tell him what happened. Reed Slater would be gone and she wouldn't have to look over her shoulder for the remainder of the drive—at least not for him.

Except, she saw the truth of the man in his eyes. She knew the look, only she'd not met anyone before now who could mask his or her true self with such skill. He would find her if she caused trouble. He would find her and do what he had planned to do tonight. Still, it was a risk she had to take. Amanda resolved that no one would have such control over her again.

10

Hawk's Peak, Montana Territory
May 1884

BEN STOPPED THE WAGON in front of the house and spoke for the first time since Amanda began her story. "Have you told anyone else?"

"Brenna knows what happened to my father and why I left Iron City."

His jaw flexed. "And Reed Slater."

"I never told anyone . . . until now." Amanda didn't know why she told Ben about Reed. It was one moment in a journey she wanted to forget. "I escaped jail. If they ever find me—"

"Don't worry about that, not now, not ever," Ben said. "Whatever they claim you've done, I know you're innocent."

He amazed her. "Just like that?" she asked.

"Just like that." Ben climbed down from the wagon seat and held a hand out for Amanda to help her down. Once both of her feet were back on solid ground, he moved to get back into the wagon. Except he waited there with the reins in his hands instead of moving the wagon forward. "None of it matters to me, Amanda."

"Ben?"

He faced her, never wavering. She always liked that about him. "I didn't blow up my father's store, and I certainly never would have harmed Bobby. I did kill a man. It was in self-defense, I know, but I had it in me to kill someone."

"We all do, Amanda. There's a difference between us and those who kill only for money or revenge, who kill without conscience."

"Have you . . ."

"Ever killed someone in revenge?"

She nodded and saw the muscle in his jaw tighten. She shouldn't have asked such a question, except she couldn't take it back. For a minute, Amanda wasn't sure he would answer.

Ben slowly nodded. "A long time ago." He said nothing else before he drove the wagon toward the barn.

AMANDA SECURED ONE END of a sheet to the drying line, careful to keep the rest in the basket at her feet. She'd convinced Catie to spend the day playing and promised Elizabeth, Brenna and Ramsey's grandmother, that she was happy to finish the laundry, and suggested she enjoy the afternoon sun on the veranda.

Amanda preferred to be alone with her thoughts right now. She loved to spend time with Elizabeth, even if half the time was spent convincing her to rest. Catie had proven to be a delightful distraction, always filled with questions and ready to absorb information, and learn new things about life, the world, and anything else they were willing to teach her.

In these quiet moments when the sun beat down on a rain-free day, Amanda found she could forget the heartache from the year before . . . except today. Ben's words mingled with Brenna's until her mind couldn't separate the well-intended advice with the fear she'd harbored for so long.

Amanda smoothed the top edge of the sheet across the line and fixed it with one of the wooden clothespins she had in her apron. The sheet flapped in the breeze, followed by the sound of a horse's snort. She turned to see Ben a few yards away on the back of a gelding she didn't recognize. His golden hair caught a glint of sunlight, even with the dark hat he always wore.

Ben dismounted and walked toward her, leaving the horse to graze nearby.

"Pretty day."

"I wondered if winter would ever end." Amanda dropped the remaining clothespins into the empty basket and checked the white kitchen cloths she'd hanged only a few minutes ago.

"We've had worse. I've spent a winter or two in Dakota and it's not any better," Ben said. "No wonder you managed so well."

Ben stood, watching her. Feeling like a coward, Amanda stopped fidgeting with the laundry basket and faced him. "About yesterday."

"That's what I came over to talk to you about."

"Oh?" Amanda tried to ease the tightness between her shoulders.

"I'm glad you told me." They both turned when the horse walked a short distance from one patch of grass to the next. Ben continued. "You said Brenna knows, and I think you should tell the rest of the family."

Amanda rubbed her hands over her folded arms, not from the cold but to give herself a few seconds before responding. "I know. I knew as soon as I told Brenna."

Ben reached out his hand but midway pulled it back, letting it fall at his side. "You suffered a great loss when your father was killed. Then you lost your home, your livelihood, and everything else familiar before they tried to take your freedom. It's good to grieve and even try and forget. You'll be better for it in the long run if you can put this behind you."

Amanda couldn't imagine ever putting her father's murder behind her. "That's not as easy done as said."

This time, Ben did touch her, placing a strong hand on her folded arm. "I don't mean put your father's death behind you. God knows, I couldn't. I meant, find out if there's even a reason to be afraid any longer."

Amanda wanted to ask him what he'd

meant about his father. Ben had shared so little of his own personal life. Instead she asked, "What are you suggesting?"

"Rather than continuing to wonder, you find out if the men who killed your father and burned down the store are actually looking for you."

"I've considered that. Only, if I were to make inquiries, they could be alerted. If they weren't looking for me before, they certainly would after. I wouldn't be surprised if they thought I died somewhere in the wilderness. I hadn't realized the difficult terrain, or the long stretch of territory I would have to travel through. I didn't think except to get as far away from there as I could."

"Would you rather continue to hide and live in fear of the unknown? You can resolve this by sharing your story with the Gallaghers. They have connections and influence that can help."

Ben's words ignited a spark within

Amanda. "I wonder if I'm strong enough for a fight, if it comes to that. I was here for only the end of the troubles this family faced because of Nathan Hunter." Amanda recalled those last days of Hunter with clarity. The destruction and fear he caused to his own flesh and blood had been abominable, and yet his grandchildren—Brenna and Ramsey—were stronger for it. "I don't know how Brenna and Isabelle and Eliza got through it all."

"You have the strength, and deep down, you know you're capable of facing whatever might come your way." He stepped closer, his voice soft yet unyielding. "You're forgetting something very important about what Brenna and the others went through."

Amanda's eyes met his. She felt his strength and more palpably, his love.

"They weren't alone, Amanda. Not for one minute, no matter if they were apart from the people they loved for a brief time. They were never alone. And neither are you."

TO AMANDA'S SURPRISE, THE whole family—minus the children—gathered at the main house for supper along with Ben. Isabelle moved with enviable ease, though the dark circles revealed the exhausting toll the pregnancy was taking on her body. Gabriel kept one hand on the small of her back whenever she wasn't sitting.

Eliza and Ramsey currently resided in their new cabin, closer to the main house, while the old ranch underwent some improvements. Andrew was tucked in the guest bed with Jacob, and thanks to Catie, enjoyed an animated bedtime story while the adults gathered downstairs in the sitting room.

A fire burned low in the hearth to help remove some of the evening chill. Amanda waited until the rest of the family had joined together in the room before stopping Ben in the hall. "Was this your idea?"

Ben didn't take offense, though Amanda chided herself for the poor delivery of the question. "This wasn't me. Ethan's the one who asked me to join the family for dinner tonight. Let's go in. We won't figure anything out by standing here."

Amanda looked at each of the faces in the room, one by one, though none betrayed anything about why they'd gathered. She couldn't help but suspect the reason was her. No matter who called the family meeting, she'd been given an opportunity.

She and Eliza had each carried a tray into the room, one with tea and the other with slices of a sweet apple cake Elizabeth had baked that afternoon. Isabelle sipped at her tea, her eyes bright with love as she looked at Gabriel. Brenna drank a little from her china cup before setting it aside and splaying her hands over her round belly. Ethan remained close to her, and Amanda noticed even the slightest twitch from Brenna, his focus would immediately shift to his wife.

Ramsey handed a glass each to Ethan and Gabriel before settling down with his own brandy. Eliza, comfortable in her surroundings, leaned against her husband's side and whispered something in Ramsey's ear, causing him to chuckle. Elizabeth sat in a rocking chair near the hearth, her shadow cast by the glow from the low-burning fire.

If a master artist sat in the room with brush and canvas, he could not paint a picture this perfect. "Since we're all here tonight, I have something I'd like to share with all of you." Amanda shifted in her chair and folded her hands in her lap. "Brenna and Ben already know, and I suspect Ethan may have some idea."

A few laughs escaped before Gabriel said, "Not much gets past him, especially if it concerns the family." He sobered. "And you're family, Amanda."

Her racing heart calmed a few degrees. "There isn't another family I'd rather belong to . . . except the one I lost."

11

Briarwood, Montana Territory
October, 1883

THE DAKOTA HILLS PALED in comparison
to the impressive mountains surrounding
the peaceful town of Briarwood. Already
topped with snow, the peaks rose above a
layer of dense clouds eager to release more
snow and rain upon the valley below.

The wagon bumped along in the
furrows, partially filled with water leftover
from the wet snow that had fallen the day
before. She studied the homes and
businesses lined up neatly along either
side of the single road leading into the
quaint, mountain township. The quiet and
well-tended street conveyed a gentleness

on the surface, and Amanda wondered if it was always this peaceful. She desperately needed to rest.

Her thoughts drifted back to the quiet, starry night when Reed Slater accosted her. Having no other choice, Amanda told the wagon master what Reed attempted to do, and would have succeeded had it not been for the other guide calling out when he did. As a Christian group, they tolerated no violence, especially toward women and children. Reed had immediately been dismissed from the party. She watched him ride away into the morning light to be certain.

When the wagons reached Bozeman, half of them decided to continue south and the other half opted to remain in the bustling town and wait out the winter. Amanda didn't want to linger in any one place longer than necessary.

She could buy a train ticket under another name and disappear, yet somehow the thought of continuing west to one of the larger cities held no appeal. Reed Slater didn't give her much of a choice about staying or going when he showed up outside the boardinghouse where she'd taken temporary lodging.

He leaned against one of the posts supporting the overhang. "We didn't get to finish what we started, Miss Warren."

The sunny afternoon had brought enough people outdoors to give Amanda some measure of comfort. "And we never will, Mr. Slater." How did she ever think he was a kind man?

"That'd be a mighty shame. I could show you a real good time."

"Stay away from me, or I'll notify the sheriff." Amanda didn't wait to around to see what else he might say or do. She closed the front door of the boardinghouse and immediately went to her room on the second floor and locked the door. She had intended to leave the following morning to find a quiet town away from the railroad, but she couldn't risk leaving now, not when there was a chance Reed might follow.

Two weeks passed and Amanda left her room only when necessary. After she saw Reed through the window loitering across the street, her fear turned to anger. The proprietor of the boardinghouse had a son of twelve years, and it was to him Amanda went with a special task. When he returned later in the day, he handed her a note with a name.

"Seven o'clock tomorrow morning near the wagon camp."

"Thank you so much for your help." Amanda pressed two silver dollars into the boy's hand. "I have one more task for you if you're willing."

The boy stared at the coins and eagerly nodded.

Amanda arrived at the wagons fifteen minutes early and waited in the nearby trees. When she was certain Reed hadn't seen her leave out the back door, or followed her, she went in search of the Duncans.

The family was pleased to accept additional payment in exchange for her passage. Amanda gave the two horses hitched to the wagon a cursory glance and decided they looked strong enough to make the rugged journey north. She turned her attention to the young couple and their two children, and although they appeared tired and a little thin, they were clean and appeared to take good care with their meager possessions.

Her father used to tell her that the character of any person could be judged by how he treats wife, children, and animals. She suffered a moment of hesitation, considering her other options. She didn't wish to remain in Bozeman, nor did she wish to continue in another direction. The train didn't go north—at least in the direction they were headed—and she considered this an advantage, hoping Sheriff Cobb, Baldwin Irving, or anyone else looking for her, wouldn't think to look for her on the outskirts of civilization.

Amanda handed the first half of the payment to the man and told him he'd receive the other half when they arrived at their destination.

He looked aghast at the amount of money she gave him. "You don't even know where we're going, Miss Warren."

"Please, call me Amanda. If you're going north, that's good enough for me." Guilt settled in her heart at the thought of leaving her father's horse behind. She considered taking him, but she didn't believe he could make the trek. The poor animal had given enough by traveling this far. He'd been a worthy companion for her father for twenty-five years. Now he deserved a rest as much as she needed one. Amanda knew the young boy who helped her get away would give him a good home.

AMANDA WOULD ALWAYS REMEMBER the week she spent traveling with the Duncans. They shared chores and enjoyed each other's company. The father told stories at night while his children listened with rapture. His wife pulled out her knitting every night and finished a new scarf for each of her children by the time they arrived in Briarwood.

A few onlookers paused in their step to wherever they were headed to catch a glimpse of the newcomers. What a sight they must be, Amanda thought. Without a decent place to freshen up, they were bedraggled from the journey and all eager for a hot bath and good night's sleep.

A sheriff's office, a livery, a small café, and a general store dominated the main road of Briarwood. A boardinghouse and saloon stood at the end of the road before it curved around, though what lay beyond, Amanda couldn't see from where they stopped.

"Where will you go now?" Clyde Duncan asked when the pulled up in front of the livery.

"Here I suppose." At least long enough to rest, Amanda thought. "And what about your family?"

"Farming, we hope. My brother has a place east of town. It's small, but I reckon with some hard work, we can make a go of it." Clyde climbed down from the high wagon seat and helped her before making his way around back to assist his family. His wife was six months along in her confinement, something Amanda hadn't known until the woman revealed it to her after a pain shot through her back.

Clyde and Helen Duncan walked back around the wagon. "They say Montana is one of the few places where a person can make anything of themselves, no matter where they come from or how much money they have." He grinned down at his wife who stood a head shorter than him. "Ain't that right, Helen?"

The woman smiled and slipped an arm around her husband. "We mean to make a new start here."

Amanda wasn't sure about a new beginning for her, but if she decided to remain in Briarwood for a time, at least she would have friends. She handed them another leather pouch with the second half of the payment, but Clyde held up a hand to stop her.

"We can't take so much. You paid more than what's fair already."

Amanda glanced at the woman heavy with child and their two young children, all who had come to begin a new life on a dream and a prayer. "Yes, you can. You've done more for me than you'll ever know. Please, take this with my blessings and gratitude."

Helen massaged her stomach and covered it with the edges of her wool shawl. "What about you?"

Amanda smiled and meant it, more than she had since the night her father bled out on the floor of his shop. "If it's true what they say about Montana, about making anything of oneself, I believe I've also come to the right place."

Amanda gathered her bag and walked toward the boardinghouse. On impulse, she veered toward the saloon. It was early enough in the morning and the interior was near empty save for a few men playing cards at a corner table.

A woman stood behind the bar and looked up when Amanda entered. "You lost, honey?"

"I don't believe so." She walked toward the bar and set her bag on one of the stools. "I'm looking for a job."

12

Hawk's Peak, Montana Territory
May 14, 1884

"I ALWAYS KNEW THERE had to be another reason why you took a job at Millie's Saloon," Eliza said.

Amanda felt heat rise into her cheeks. "How I must have looked to you that day."

"I know the Duncans."

Amanda looked up at Ben who stood by her chair. "Clyde and Helen. They're still here?"

Ben nodded. "I've helped Clyde take supplies out to the farm he and his brother are working."

"I worried they might not make it through the winter, but I should have known. They were resilient and so optimistic about their future here."

She turned back to face the rest of the group. "I want to apologize for not telling you the full story before now. I left a few pieces of the story out when I spoke with Brenna and Ben. Now you have the whole of it."

The questions began, and the family was careful not to overwhelm her. Ethan had remained silent throughout and seemed content to let Ramsey ask the first question.

"Do you suspect both the sheriff and the deputy in Iron City?"

"I don't know. The deputy, Isaac Porter, never gave me any reason to suspect him until the night he helped me escape, but I can't be certain what he meant. I knew Isaac—Porter—well enough to believe he wasn't involved in my father's death. What else he might have done for Mr. Irving, I don't want to speculate. I've no doubt

Sheriff Cobb was somehow involved, but I didn't have a chance to find out how much."

Gabriel spoke next. "Is Porter the type of man who would cover for the sheriff?"

Amanda opened her mouth to speak only to realize she didn't know. "I'm not sure."

"Getting out of there was your first priority. You did the right thing." Ben moved an empty chair from against the wall and set it down beside Amanda.

Isabelle moved to the edge of the settee and leaned against Gabriel. "It's been nine months since you left. Have you seen anything during that time that would make you believe they're looking for you?"

"No, which is why I feel foolish for worrying so much. If it weren't for my . . . escape, but there's more. I never did find out what happened to Bobby. The guilt of not knowing has weighed more heavily than the fear."

"It's hardly an escape when you were unjustly accused and imprisoned," Ethan said when he joined the conversation. "It's not foolish, especially after what you went through. You've been here awhile now, though. What's happened recently to increase your worry?"

Amanda stared at Ethan, uncertain how he managed to know the root of the problem.

Brenna grinned and said, "I told you, he knows everything that happens around here."

"You're correct in believing my worry has increased, but not for any reason you might think. Nothing has happened. When I first arrived, there was too much to occupy my thoughts. Between . . ." She looked to Brenna.

"It's all right. You mean my grandfather."

Amanda nodded. "Between Hunter and then Catie coming along at Christmas, I didn't have time to think about myself. I was grateful to keep busy. When I started going into town a few days a week, I saw the people coming and going and suddenly found myself wondering if one of the newcomers or someone passing through would be Sheriff Cobb."

Ramsey leaned forward, resting his arms on his legs. To many he would appear relaxed, but his eyes, a mirror of Brenna's, held a seriousness Amanda didn't often see. "I imagine Ben has already said something similar, but if you want to put this matter to rest, we need to make inquiries and find out what really happened to your father, and if there's a warrant circulating for your arrest."

"About my father? I know what happened."

Ramsey shook his head and scooted forward a little more. "You know he was murdered by this Barker, and you suspect the sheriff was involved along with the banker. To truly give you peace, we need to find your father's killer or killers. In the meantime, we'll make some other inquiries about the boy—Bobby. It shouldn't be too difficult to find out if a young boy in a small town—"

"Died," Amanda whispered. The truth, no matter what it may be, would be better than not knowing. Her father deserved justice and she deserved a life without looking over her shoulder and wondering. "What should I do first?"

"Nothing." Ramsey sat back in the chair and twined his fingers with Eliza's. "I'll make the inquiries and let you know if anything comes of it."

"And if no one is looking for me?"

"Let's see what my inquiries bring first before we decide on the next steps. The law is most likely on your side, Amanda, regardless of why the sheriff arrested you. A man like him doesn't represent the laws of the territory, especially when it appears he's taking orders from Mr. Irving."

"I remember the difficulties all of you went through to get justice. It wasn't easy, but you did what had to be done and I can't do any less. I'm grateful to you all for not judging me and for your help. I'm only sorry I waited to so long to come forward."

BEN WAITED UNTIL THE family members had said their good nights before he stepped outside. The evening stars burned brightly and the constellations told a story centuries old. He often looked up at those formations when the night was darkest and the cries from inside the cabin were loudest.

When he left home at sixteen years, he couldn't have known what awaited him in the world. No matter where he ended up, he could gaze into the starry sky and for a few moments, ignore the chaos.

"Ben?"

He turned, the painful memories

washed away by the sight of her. Amanda didn't often loosen her hair but now it flowed freely over her shoulders. The oat-colored tresses glimmered beneath the moonlight and he caught the faintest touch of red. Her dewy skin held a hint of the sun. He'd never seen or known anyone so beautiful.

Ben cleared his throat. "Pretty night."

She nodded and walked toward him to sit on the edge of the railing. "When I was younger, my family lived in Pennsylvania. I could see the stars, but nothing ever like the glory of them out here."

"Do you still have family back east?"

"Some. An aunt and uncle and a few cousins on my mother's side I met as a young girl. My mother wasn't close with them, which I suppose made it easier for her to venture west with my father. It's not home and hasn't been for a long time." She turned away from the stars and looked at him. "Do you have family somewhere beyond Hawk's Peak?"

"Not anymore." Ben hadn't spoken of his past in over a decade. Amanda wasn't the only one who tried to forget. "An older couple took me in when I was sixteen and raised me as their own, even sent me to college. They passed a few years ago."

"What about . . . never mind."

Ben joined her on the railing and leaned against the post. "After everything you've shared, you've earned the right to ask a few questions of your own. Go ahead, ask."

"It's different."

"Maybe. Maybe not. We all have stories and secrets. Some are easier to share than others, and some cut too deep that we'd just as soon forget them."

"Have you forgotten?"

"Some memories can't be buried."

A frigid breeze crept up on them, lifting the edges of Amanda's hair. "Is a storm coming?"

More than one, Ben thought. "We'll

have rain before morning. We can get snow in these mountains well into summer. I left home not long before Marge and Josiah Allen took me in."

Amanda accepted the uttered admission in stride, for which he was grateful. "You didn't take their name."

Ben shook his head and looked back up at the sky where clouds began to darken the moon's light. "Stuart is my mother's family name. She died a week after my sixteenth birthday. It was the only way I knew how at the time to honor her." He faced Amanda and saw she remained focused on him. "I can't go back and change what happened to my family, and I can only pray my mother is resting in peace. I will do all I can to help you find justice for yours. I promise."

"You believe Ramsey will be successful?"

Ben perused her lovely face and nodded. "When Gallaghers get it in their heads to do something, not much deters them."

Amanda's fingers splayed over her throat only to tug the edges of her shawl together. "In other words, when you say Ramsey will succeed, I'm to believe it may not be good news."

Ben leaned in, his focus on anything else but her forgotten. "If you had to do it all over again, would you, no matter the result?"

"Yes."

"In your mind then and now, there was something or someone to fear. Unease doesn't come out of nowhere."

It was Amanda who reached out to touch him. Though the weight of her hand was slight, his skin warmed. "The unease is not so terrifying at this moment."

13

HEAVY RAINS AND THUNDER lasted the evening and crept into the morning hours. The torrent left the vegetable garden in disarray and offered up a new distraction for Amanda. She deepened a furrow alongside a row of seedlings, allowing the excess water to drain into the surrounding earth.

As she dug the hoe into the ground and delighted in the simple springtime task, Catie and Andrew worked with smaller implements to dig their own grooves in the bed and gently pat dirt around the base of the seedlings. They didn't miss the chance to play a little in the mud, as attested by the occasional giggle.

For a few seconds, Amanda tilted her head back and allowed the midday sun to kiss her skin. More rain would come to brighten the already brilliant green fields and give sustenance to the wild prairie grass they would harvest later for hay to feed the horses and cattle during the long winters.

Ranch life had seemed so complex when Amanda moved in with the Gallaghers, but in reality it was a simple cycle of hard work, weather, and determination. The cycle continued year after year in a natural revolution that she had not fully appreciated until she came to Hawk's Peak.

The sound of horses interrupted her quiet enjoyment. She turned to see Ramsey and Ben ride toward the fenced-in garden. Catie, shrewd beyond her thirteen years, glanced once at the men, then at Amanda.

"Andrew, why don't we get cleaned up and see if Grandma Hunter will let us into the cookie tin?" Catie rose and shook out her skirt and apron the best she could.

"Do you think she has molasses?" Andrew asked when he stood to join her.

"Maybe, and oatmeal. Those are my favorite."

The children walked toward the house, leaving Amanda to wait for the men. Ben and Ramsey both dismounted and walked toward her. Neither appeared ready to deliver good news.

Amanda met them at the fence. "You've heard something?"

Ramsey kept his horse's reins in one hand and rested the other on a post. "It's not the news I had hoped to bring you. At least not all of it. Bobby Ross is alive."

"Then he wasn't in the store when it burned?"

"Nearby. He ran from the store when the fire started, but hit his head and fell under some rubble. He was injured, but recovered." Ramsey placed a hand on her shoulder. "He's all right, Amanda."

The pressure around Amanda's heart eased a little more . . . until Ramsey continued.

"Your initial instincts were right, Amanda. Sheriff Cobb has made some discreet inquiries about you."

Amanda chest tightened. "Is he getting close?"

"No." Ben's manner reflected none of the worry Amanda felt, but his eyes held a quiet violence. "His search went in an easterly direction. He checked with a sheriff he knows in Cheyenne, but he hasn't reached out to anyone closer, at least as far as we know."

The constriction in her stomach eased. "Then there is time to learn the truth before he finds me."

"It won't be that easy."

Amanda's gaze shifted from Ben to

Ramsey. "What do you mean?"

"Sheriff Cobb is missing."

ONE WEEK PASSED WITHOUT incident, and Amanda refused to be held prisoner by herself or her fears. Catie wanted to participate in rehearsals for the spring play the schoolchildren planned to put on in two weeks, and Amanda wanted to drive her. It hadn't been easy to convince Brenna and Elizabeth that she wasn't in need of an escort. If Ethan and the other men hadn't already been out with the cattle or at other various chores, they might have won the argument.

Amanda stepped down from the wagon one of the men hitched up for her that morning and a smile touched her lips when Catie nearly jumped from the seat to the grass below. Wildflowers dotted the meadow beyond the school, and a small herd of deer pranced into the trees when a group of children ran through the tall grass in a game of chase.

A shout from the front door of the schoolhouse reached them. "Hello, Miss Warren!" Cord Beckert waved and ran to close the short distance between them. "Hi, Catie."

"Hi, Cord." A soft, rose hue tinted Catie's cheeks.

Amanda delighted to watch the friendship and affection grow between them. When she had first met Cord before Christmas, he and his mother barely had food in their cupboards or a roof over their head. Cord now displayed the health and vitality of a young man who had the chance at a good life.

Though neither Ben or Colton, Hawk's Peak top tracker, had admitted to helping secure the mother and son a new home in town, she believed it to be the truth. Cord's mother, Sarah, found a job at Tilly's café, and she now thrived. Life wasn't easy, but Amanda imagined the new circumstances were close to perfect for the small family.

Cord's countenance brightened with his smile when he said to Catie. "Mrs. Carver said you and me can direct the play."

"You and I," Amanda corrected him. "That sounds like a wonderful idea." She lifted the basket of cookies she and Elizabeth had made that morning out of the back. "Catie, why don't you take these in with you, and I'll return after I've seen to filling my list at the general store."

Cord and Catie, walking with heads close enough to whisper, giggled and disappeared with the cookies into the schoolhouse.

Amanda climbed back into the wagon and drove down Briarwood's single street to the general store. With list in hand, she grabbed her shopping basket and walked inside.

"Good day to you, Amanda."

"Good morning, Joanna. I have an order to place with Loren. Is he about?"

Joanna brushed back a stand of gray hair and secured it into the bun at her nape. "Poor dear isn't feeling himself today. I can place your order."

Amanda passed her the carefully penned list Brenna had given her in the morning. "I'm afraid Brenna found quite a few items she wanted for the new baby. Isabelle has the catalog now."

Joanna's chuckled softly when she perused the list. "She's going to have the best-dressed baby in Montana."

"She wanted to come in herself, but the wagon ride isn't too comfortable for her these days."

"It won't be long now, will it?"

Amanda set the basket on the counter and relaxed. She enjoyed the normalcy of having a conversation with the storekeeper's wife. Next she would purchase a few items for a cake she wished to try, and then she would watch the children rehearse at the school. Simple.

Normal was all she wanted today. "A month still, I'd guess. Their husbands are showing more impatience than Brenna and Isabelle."

"Isn't that men. None of the work and still they get frazzled." Joanna grinned, causing the laugh lines around her mouth to deepen. She was a handsome woman and as kind and generous as her husband. "Loren was beside himself when our girl was born. We had her so late in our life, but all worked out. Poor man fainted when the time came."

"I didn't realize you had a daughter."

"She was only seventeen when she got it in her head to head out east and go to one of those fancy schools and see the Atlantic Ocean. An adventurer, that's our Keera. Married two years back . . . I can hardly believe it."

"Do you visit her?"

"We went for the wedding, in Maine of all places. A grand affair if ever I saw one.

She married well, our girl."

"She's a lucky woman, your daughter." Amanda noticed sadness touch Joanna's features and quickly changed the subject. "I have a few other items I need to pick up and I'll have a look at your new fabric while I'm here. It's time I make myself a new dress."

AMANDA LEFT THE STORE with her purchases and found Catie and Cord speaking quietly together by the wagon. Cord hurried to retrieve the bundles from Amanda's arms and slid them into the wagon.

"Thank you, Cord."

Though a year younger than Catie, he stood a few inches taller. Amanda marveled at how he'd changed and grown in the months since she first met him. She saw in him a bright young man, who with some guidance—provided by a few of the men from the ranch—would grow into a wonderful person. And the world could use more, she thought. "You're done early. I wanted to watch." Amanda secured the back of the wagon and adjusted the wide-brimmed hat she'd taken to wearing in the last few months.

"The teacher said we did such a good job, and it was too pretty to be inside all day." Catie held up a thin booklet. "The older kids get to take home a copy of the play so they can practice lines, but I don't have to because I'm the director."

"That's a very important job. And what about you, Cord? What job did the teacher give you?"

He stood proudly and said, "I get to help build the set and direct with Catie. Do you think maybe Ben and Colton might want to help?"

"I can't speak for either of them, but it doesn't hurt to ask." Amanda believed both would readily agree to help however they could. Neither man was the social type, but she'd realized when it came to helping others, everyone at Hawk's Peak was willing to give of their time. "Catie, we'll need to head back to the ranch soon, but since you've finished early, how about a piece of pie for each of us from Tilly's?"

Both children were enthusiastic in their agreement. Amanda found she enjoyed their company as much as she did any adult's. Catie was bright and eager to learn, and Cord possessed a natural intelligence, which would serve him well.

Their laughter over a story Cord told them about rabbit hunting followed them from Tilly's café. The sun beat down upon them and yet a chill caressed Amanda's skin, only it began from within. She surveyed the street and the windows in the buildings across the way. Otis stood outside his blacksmith shop and waved when he noticed them. The children waved back, and Amanda managed a smile, but the cold had reached her blood.

"Come along, Cord, your mother will begin to wonder where you are." The children loaded into the wagon while Amanda once more scanned their surroundings.

There, in front of the swinging saloon doors, stood the source of the biting cold coursing through Amanda. She squinted and focused, unsure if it was deception from the sun or if her nightmare had finally come to Briarwood. He raised his head and their eyes met.

No deception, no mistake. Sheriff Stratton Cobb wasn't missing—he was hunting.

14

"WHAT'S WRONG, AMANDA?"
Catie's voice broke through and Amanda climbed into the wagon to join them on the seat.

"Nothing to worry about. I thought I saw someone I once knew." Amanda checked beneath the seat where a rifle waited within reach. She turned once more to look for Cobb, but no one stood in the saloon's doorway this time, and she saw no sign of him on the streets. With her back to the saloon, she drove the wagon toward Cord's house.

The tidy home had been transformed just like its occupants. Hard work and generosity had gone into turning the dilapidated structure into a safe and clean home. She pulled the team to a stop in front of the house and Cord jumped down.

"Didn't expect to see anyone else from the ranch in town today."

Amanda automatically reached for the gun before she realized how foolish she must look.

"I didn't mean to startle you, Amanda." Colton's horse stopped alongside the wagon. Instead of asking about her behavior, he tipped the edge of his hat to Catie and waved to Cord who headed inside.

"You didn't startle me."

"You're white as the clean sheets hanging out to dry," Catie said.

"What a lovely thought," Amanda replied dryly. "It's time we headed back."

"I've finished up for the day here."

Colton rested his arms on the pommel of the saddle, and though he said nothing,

Amanda suspected he saw plenty.

"If you don't mind the company, I'll join you."

"We wouldn't mind at all, would we, Amanda?" Catie asked.

Amanda clicked her tongue and lightly tapped the long, leather reins over the horses' rumps. "We most certainly wouldn't."

Amanda peered around Catie as they set in motion toward the opposite side of town and the road which would lead them home. "Can you tell us a story, Mr. Dawson? Brenna says you have lots of them."

Amanda sensed Colton regarding her even as he obliged Catie and told a tale of the time he had to outsmart a pack of wolves. Amanda only hoped she'd be smart enough to do likewise when the time came.

"I'M TELLING YOU, BEN, something wasn't

right with her today."

Ben and Colton had finished up supper and opted to spend the last two hours of daylight working on the addition to the bunkhouse. It was already spacious enough to comfortably fit the ranch hands, each with their own room, but the Gallaghers were always in favor of improving the ranch—and the lives of those who called it home—whenever possible.

He'd spoken with Ethan a few days before about buying a corner of Hawk's Peak land so he could build his own cabin. Ben had no desire to leave the ranch or build his life somewhere else.

Ben set his hammer down in one of the wooden boxes that held their tools. "What happened?"

"I don't know. I spoke before she saw it was me, and she reached for the rifle under the seat." Colton put away the extra nails and planted his hat back on his head.

"I don't know what's going on, and I don't need to know, but I'd wager my horse something has been bothering Amanda—and you."

Ben drank from the canteen he'd hung on a nearby peg before answering. "She ever talk about her past with you?"

"Not in too many words. I figure she has one considering the way she ended up here, but I haven't asked her about it." Colton's eyes narrowed as he scrutinized Ben. "Does she need help?"

It didn't matter what the circumstances, Ben knew Colton would be there. Like many of the men who wandered onto Hawk's Peak and chose to stay, Colton didn't speak much about his life before. Ben was no different. Only Ethan knew about Ben's history, and not every detail. Times past were not where Ben wanted to live, and Amanda's own story had raised issues he'd thought buried deep inside a long time ago.

"She might. Ramsey's looking into something for her." It was her story to tell, and yet sharing it with Colton is what felt right in that moment. Ben didn't reveal everything personal, but in the evening hours as the sun began to set over the peaks and the men inside the bunkhouse enjoyed a game of cards, Ben told Colton about Sheriff Cobb.

DINNER HAD BEEN AN enjoyable affair for the small family after which Catie tried to teach young Jacob how to say "wolf," but it came out as "wool." When he attempted to say her name, it came out as "Cat."

"He'll get it soon enough." Brenna lifted Jacob into her arms and kissed his forehead. "It's time for bed now. Would you like to do a bit of reading?"

"I want to read the play the teacher let me take home. I need to bring it back when I go into town next." Catie folded the afghan she'd been using and set it on the chair. "Amanda said she could help me."

"I'm sure she will." Brenna bounced her son on her hip and smiled when he said "mama." "I haven't seen Amanda since dinner."

"I don't think she's up for company. Maybe it was her friend."

Brenna paused in her play with Jacob. "Whose friend?"

The girl shrugged. "Amanda said she thought she saw someone today. She didn't seem too happy afterward."

"I see." Brenna pressed another kiss to her son' s cheek and tweaked his nose. "Let's get this little one to bed and you can read for a bit."

Brenna and Catie made their way up the stairs to the second level of the spacious house. When she had moved to Hawk's Peak, the Gallagher siblings all lived at the ranch. They filled almost every bedroom, and Brenna had wondered how they would all manage when Isabelle and

Andrew joined them, and then Ramsey. Now that half of the family lived under their own roofs, Hawk's Peak was a quiet place and there were days when Brenna missed having everyone there.

However, once in a while the privacy was exactly what she needed. Once Jacob was settled in for the evening, Brenna went downstairs and walked onto the front porch. She welcomed the cool night air and savored the scent of fresh pine.

"I was hoping you'd join me." Ethan stepped away from the railing and walked toward her, his arms circling her pregnant waist in an unhurried motion. "Everyone else asleep?"

Brenna leaned into her husband, tension easing from her body as it always did when she was in his arms. "Grandmother retired an hour ago and I've just put Jacob down. Catie's reading in bed. I came looking for Amanda."

"And here I thought it was me that

brought you out here."

She teased him back with a leisurely kiss. "I always know where I can find you." Her brow furrowed, concern etched across her face. "Something Catie said tonight . . . I'd like to speak with Amanda and I think you should be there."

Ethan sobered. "She was quiet at dinner. Do you know if anything has happened?"

"No. I just want her to know we're here for her, no matter what, and that she can always come to us." Brenna smoothed her hand over Ethan's heart, and he covered her hand.

"I know." Amanda stood beneath the moon's glow, a shawl wrapped over her shoulders, her fingers toying with the wool edges. "If you have a few minutes, I'd like your advice."

"Of course." Brenna walked down the steps to meet her.

"I'll meet you inside shortly." Ethan

stood at the stop of the steps. Amanda wondered what drew his attention, but she saw only the distant mountains.

"Ethan?" Brenna's soft accent filled the quiet night silence.

"I'll be right along." He pressed a kiss to her cheek and waited for them to go inside.

Over her shoulder, Amanda caught the concern etched in Ethan's expression and wondered what had caught his interest.

ETHAN COVERED THE DISTANCE to the corrals in unhurried steps. The moon's light cast enough of a glow to guide him as he made his way around the back of the barn, past the chicken coop, and into the field of spring grass.

A breeze swept across the meadow, bringing with it the scent of pine and cattle. Ethan listened to the familiar sounds of the ranch and stared across the expanse to the trees and over the gentle slopes before they evened out and wended their way into the base of the mountains.

He knew every tree, rock, and blade of grass on his land, but most importantly, he sensed when something had disturbed the energy—the life force—of the ranch. All was quiet except for the gentle whish of the breeze, the babbling of the stream, and the lone cry of a wolf far enough in the distance not to cause concern.

"You hear that?"

Ethan nodded but didn't turn when Ben walked up beside him. The crunch of Ben's boots on a twig had given him away. "They're far enough away not to give us trouble, at least tonight."

Ben asked, "You see something else?"

"No, just a feeling." Ethan glanced at the foreman who had become a friend. They considered everyone who worked at the ranch as part of their family. Ethan knew Ben and Colton better than he did the others. He always sensed that he had more in common with them. When Ben first arrived looking for a job doing whatever they might need, Ethan had wondered what brought an educated, former lawman to a ranch in the middle of Montana. He hadn't pried when Ben hired on, but he suspected there was more to the man than he wanted the world to see. It was years later when Ethan managed to get a few details out of him, and only then because Ben was half delirious from an injury.

Ethan developed a deeper respect for Ben after that, for any man who was strong enough to overcome his demons and make something of his life, deserved regard. Ethan didn't have the whole story—he didn't need it—and he suspected Ben would eventually share it with Amanda, if he hadn't already.

"You were a lawman once," Ethan said, now that he faced Ben. "If you were in Cobb's place, what would your next move be?"

Ben didn't hesitate to say, "I'd already be here. If I wanted to find Amanda, I would have found her, and if Cobb was any good at his job, he would've shown up by now."

"Could be he's not good at finding people, or Amanda did a great job of covering her tracks."

"Based on what Amanda's told us, I'd say she did a very good job of misdirecting them, but I wouldn't say Cobb is stupid."

Ethan considered and then asked, "Then why the delay? It's been almost a year and it wouldn't take that long to get from Dakota to here."

"Unless the delay was intentional on Cobb's part," Ben said. "To be honest, I want him to show up, and if he doesn't soon, I just might go looking for him."

ETHAN, GABRIEL, AND ELIZA sat atop their horses and looked out over the vast landscape of Hawk's Peak. The main house the elder Jacob Gallagher had originally built for his family was now the bunkhouse. After a few years of hard work, the house they lived in now was built. With the exception of updates to accommodate their version of indoor plumbing, the house had remained unchanged.

Gabriel and Isabelle's home now stood not far across the year-round stream, and the cabin Ramsey and Eliza built remained hidden in the trees, just as they seemed to prefer. Although there were times when Ethan missed having his siblings under one roof, he was grateful for the extra space now that his own family was growing—and if fate was on their side—would continue to grow.

The new stable now accommodated the expanding-breeding operation, which is where Eliza and Ramsey spent most of their time—except today. Ethan rode up to this spot every so often as a reminder of both responsibility and humility for what they'd been entrusted with and what their children would one day inherit.

Today, he had asked Eliza and Gabriel to join him and not just out of sentimentality. The discussion with Amanda the night before had been brief and primarily took place between Amanda and Brenna while he listened and answered when asked a question. In the end, it had simply been family sharing their thoughts, fears, and offering support.

Amanda had slowly become like a second sister to Ethan, which is why he wanted to speak with the only other two people alive who'd been there since the beginning, whose sweat, dreams, and tears covered this land.

"It's been too long since I've ridden up this way." Eliza rode astride, simple enough to do wearing the clothes she preferred when working. One year she'd managed to go through half a dozen split riding skirts, in the end resorting to pants she'd custom-ordered to fit her.

"You've been busy." Gabriel tilted his hat up a little and looked at his sister. "I stopped by the stable this morning. The horses look great."

"The stallion we bought from the Tremaines is exactly what we needed. The offspring should be strong, sound, and durable." During Eliza's quest to locate Ramsey, she'd traveled to Kentucky— unbeknownst to her brothers—where she met the Tremaines. It was from their horse farm they purchased some prime stock to help build the new herd at Hawk's Peak.

"Have you and Ramsey decided what you're doing with the old house?" Ethan asked.

Eliza nodded. "We've talked it over a few times, but we've decided not to tear it down and build new. In the end, a house is just a house. It's the people who make it a home, and Ramsey wants to see something good come from the misery Nathan Hunter brought down on everyone."

"What about Elizabeth?" Gabriel asked. "She still hasn't been back there."

"I know, and we thought about that, too. The thing is, her memories—and her pain—are different than Ramsey's. He left because he hated Hunter, who barely acknowledged his existence except as a hired hand. But it's still a part of his history—our history. This is something he needs to do, and I support him in it."

Ethan's slow nod matched his expanding smile. "I'm glad for you both, and of your decision. And don't worry about Elizabeth. She lived a good life for a lot of years up north, and from what Brenna has told me, she's put it behind her."

"That's a relief. Besides, we won't be living there."

Ethan and Gabriel both turned to her in

surprise.

"What do you mean?" Gabriel asked.

"We don't want to tear it down, but neither of us wants to live there, either. The house is a part of this ranch, and we'll take care of it, keep it up, and it will be there for the next generation. God knows we're going to need the room." Eliza winked at her brothers. "Ramsey and I spend so much time with the horses right now, and the cabin we built suits us perfectly. When we need to build on, we will."

Ethan moved his horse a little closer to Eliza's and slipped an arm over her shoulders. "You make me proud, little sister."

"Same here, big brother."

Gabriel looked on, love and pride in his family overwhelming him. It wasn't often just the three of them spent time alone these days, and he missed the camaraderie. He could see the others did as well. "At the risk of breaking up such a touching moment—ow."

Eliza grinned as Gabriel rubbed the spot on his arm she'd just punched, knowing the action was for her benefit. "It doesn't hurt."

"No, but maybe stop working so hard. You're too strong for a girl." Gabriel grinned back and then looked around her to Ethan. "All right, Ethan, I'm glad you brought us up here, but you had another reason than this little reunion."

"I wanted to talk to you about Amanda," Ethan said.

"What about her?" Eliza asked. "Has something happened?"

"No, she's holding up pretty well considering her recent revelations and knowing someone is looking for her. I don't know what she'll decide to do once she's settled the open issues from her past, but I do know she wants to stay here at Hawk's Peak."

"Of course she does," Eliza said. "She's family now. And once Ben gets around to telling her how he feels, the sooner we can start planning the wedding."

"You know about that?" Gabriel shook his head. "Of course you do."

"Gabe, everyone knows. I'd wager even Amanda knows."

Ethan nodded and looked toward the house. "And Ben is giving her time to figure out what she wants, at least according to Brenna. Ben asked me about buying a piece of land on the ranch so he can build a house. The fact is, I want to give him the land and I want to be sure the both of you agree."

"Of course he should have the land, but what does this have to do with . . ." Gabriel's attention shifted. "Did you see that light?"

Neither Ethan nor Eliza had been looking in the same direction as Gabriel, but they both turned now to look west toward a rise in the pasture.

ETHAN AND HIS SIBLINGS

speak to convey what each of them would do. Gabriel and Eliza made a wide berth, circling around while Ethan rode directly toward the rise, twilight upon them, giving them an advantage. Ethan trained the barrel of his rifle on the stranger who had a looking glass pointed toward the ranch.

"I don't suppose I can convince you to turn around and forget you saw me. I'll make it worth your while."

Ethan kept enough distance between them to give him the advantage, but not so much that he couldn't drop the man with one shot. "Unfortunately for you, I don't s, and my men wouldn't

e stranger put the looking glass saddlebags. "Then you're one of allaghers. I'm not here to harm one."

"Good to know, but you still have to answer for your trespassing." Ethan waited while the man looked around him, noticing Gabriel and Eliza, their guns also trained on him. "When a person comes onto our land and doesn't announce himself, we have to assume he's here to cause trouble. Who are you?"

"I'm looking for someone, and I was told she lived here. It's important I find her."

"Well, hell, you're Stratton Cobb."

Cobb didn't mask his surprise. "Miss Kelly told you about me."

Eliza stopped her horse a dozen feet away while Gabriel flanked Cobb. "How did you find her?"

"Word travels in certain circles. A deputy of a sheriff warned me someone had made inquiries, though I couldn't figure out why a U.S. Marshal would be looking for me."

"Which doesn't explain how you found her," Ethan said.

Cobb ignored the others and continued to watch Ethan. "I'm not here to hurt her, but I do need to find her."

"Why?" This was asked by Gabriel, whose horse now stood only a few feet from Cobb.

"That's my business."

Ethan would just as soon ride Stratton Cobb into Briarwood, lock him up, and wire the marshal, but that wasn't his decision to make. Amanda deserved to face the man she believed killed her father.

"All right, Cobb. We'll ride in, but don't think for a second we'll hesitate to shoot."

Cobb touched the brim of his hat and nodded. "I wouldn't expect otherwise."

A FEW OF THE ranch hands finishing up for the night paused in their tasks to watch the Gallaghers ride in with the stranger. They'd welcomed their fair share of strangers onto the ranch, and even a few at gunpoint, but the last time had been since before Christmas, when Catie's father had come looking for her.

"That's far enough." They stopped a few yards away from the hitching post in front of the house. Ethan turned to his sister. "Will you tell—"

Hurried footsteps drew their attention before the front door swung open. Amanda's sudden appearance outside surprised everyone as much as theirs surprised her. Ethan and Eliza were still in their saddles. Gabriel stood beside his horse, his back to her. Amanda called out to Ethan and rushed forward, only to be brought up short when she saw the gun Gabriel had trained on another man who stood behind them, until now hidden by Gabriel's height.

"You're a difficult woman to find, Miss Kelly, or is it Warren now?"

Amanda stepped to the railing. "You should have stayed in Iron City, Sheriff Cobb."

"You might feel differently after you hear why I've come."

Every urge in Amanda compelled her to walk up to Stratton Cobb and put a bullet in him herself. But there wasn't time for that. She rushed down the stairs to Ethan's side. "Brenna needs a doctor. Elizabeth is with her now."

Ethan didn't even ask for details. He dismounted with such speed, he startled his horse, and tossed the reins to Eliza before dashing into the house.

Eliza's ever-wise eyes took one look at Amanda's face and seemed to know what was happening. "Where's Ramsey?"

"I took his lunch to the stables earlier

when he didn't come in."

Eliza spun her horse around and called over her shoulder. "We'll get the doc here as soon as we can."

Amanda watched her ride away. She turned at once to face Gabriel. "What's he doing here?"

Gabriel motioned for Jake, one of the ranch hands who had been walking back from the corrals. "Take him to the barn and don't let him out of your sight. I'll send someone to sit with you and bring supper from the house."

"You got it, Gabe." Jake stood half a head shorter than Cobb, but he didn't have any trouble hauling the larger man to the barn.

Once they'd gone, Gabriel turned back to Amanda. "We found him out a ways, looking toward the ranch. There's too much going on right now to explain except to say we all thought you should have the chance to face Cobb and find out the truth.

I'm sorry," he said when he noticed her moist eyes.

Amanda swiped a hand across her cheek, wiping away a single tear. "Don't worry, I'm not afraid of him, not any longer. Seeing him brought back images from the night my father died. I'm more angry at this point than anything."

"Is Brenna having the baby?" Gabriel titled his head back as though to see through the walls of the second level.

"I don't know. It's too soon." Amanda didn't miss the concern in Gabriel's stormy-blue eyes, though she suspected the worry was for more than Brenna. "How has Isabelle been?"

"Tired. These past few weeks haven't been easy for her. She's okay, though. Between you, Catie, and Elizabeth stopping by regularly, she's doing just fine."

Amanda had come to love Gabriel as a brother and his wife as a sister. *How did she get so lucky to find this family?* "Go to Isabelle. There's nothing you can do here except worry about Brenna, and you don't need to see Ethan in this condition. I would caution you not to tell Isabelle about Brenna just yet. We don't know what's going on."

"Is it really that bad?"

"It's your brother who is likely to be more of a mess. Brenna comes from tough Highland stock; remember that."

Gabriel nodded absently. "I don't want to leave Isabelle alone right now."

"And you shouldn't. Eliza and Ramsey won't be long. Andrew came over to play earlier. He can sleep here tonight."

"Thank you, Amanda."

Amanda waited until Gabriel remounted, the reins of Ethan's horse in his hands. She watched him hand the stallion's reins to one of the men before he headed for home.

Strands of her oat-colored hair

fluttered in the evening breeze as her soft, brown eyes shifted direction to fall upon the barn. Within those walls was the man she believed responsible for her father's death, and yet she could not find the will to face him just now. She turned and made a hasty entrance into the house where a scream echoed off the walls.

BRENNA'S MOANS MATCHED THE writhing movements of her body.

Ethan's eyes met Amanda's across the length of the bed. "It's too soon for the baby." He reached for Elizabeth's arm. "Can you stop it?"

The beads of slick perspiration on Brenna's skin indicated the pain was as fierce as Ethan's fear. "Eliza fetched Ramsey to go with her into town. They'll return with the doctor as soon as they can."

Ethan's hand cupped his wife's face. He leaned close to Brenna and whispered something that brought a faint smile to her lips.

Amanda treasured these moments she witnessed between them, only the moment didn't last. Another scream wrenched through the air.

"What else can I do? I have to do something."

Without looking away from Brenna, Elizabeth said, "We'll need a fresh bowl of water, more cloths, my box of herbs, and a kettle of hot water. You know where my sewing shears are, and bring up a bottle of whiskey."

"I won't be long." Amanda found Catie standing in the hallway, terror written clearly on her young face. "Catie?"

"Andrew woke up but then went back to sleep. Jacob hasn't stirred. I want to help."

After a second of indecision, Amanda nodded. "I could use the help, but then you have to go back with the children." The last thing Amanda wanted was for Catie to see her surrogate mother in such terrible pain.

Ten minutes later, they'd gathered what they needed and made their way back upstairs. "Catie, please leave those items here in the hall and go back with the children. Thank you for your help."

Catie stared at the closed bedroom door. Brenna's moans now softer yet still loud enough to hear. "Is she going to be all right?"

"Do you know anyone stronger than Brenna?"

Catie's head shook, her light brown curls swishing over her shoulders. "No one at all."

"There you have it. I promise to get you as soon as the baby comes."

Amanda waited until Catie disappeared into the nursery before opening the door. It took two armfuls to get everything into the bedroom. Ethan hadn't budged from his place beside Brenna.

"Ethan, perhaps you should wait

downstairs."

"I'm not leaving. I don't give a damn about what's proper. I was there for Jacob's birth in Scotland and I'll be here for this one."

Amanda and Elizabeth shared a knowing look before Elizabeth joined her. "The fire is nice and hot. Set the shears near the bottom and then when I ask, pour hot water over them and bring them to the bed."

"Is the baby really coming tonight? She's not due for another month at least."

Elizabeth's expression was grim now that her back was to her granddaughter. "It is. I've delivered a few babies in my time, but I pray Doc Brody arrives before the little one."

"What's the whiskey for?"

Elizabeth tilted her head toward Ethan. "He'll need it sooner than he thinks." Elizabeth poured some of the liquid into a glass. "See this is set on the table near him." Amanda sensed the older woman's intent perusal of her. Elizabeth asked her, "You've not seen a birthing before, have you? If the doc doesn't get here on time, I may need your help."

"Don't worry about me." Amanda felt useless when Elizabeth returned to the bed. Useless and queasy. She understood now why most unmarried women remained on the other side of the door.

ANOTHER HOUR OF LABOR and a few more trips to the kitchen to refresh the water, and Elizabeth told Amanda the baby was coming. Amanda waited, ready to hand her what Elizabeth might need. As much as she loved Brenna, there were a dozen places Amanda would rather be at this moment.

The pain seemed to tear Brenna apart.

Heavy footsteps sounded in the hallway and seconds later the door thrust open. Doc Brody's large frame filled the doorway. "I hear we have a wee bairn anxious to join us."

He quickly reached the bedside where Elizabeth was preparing to deliver the baby. "Appears you have things under control, but would you like a little help?"

Elizabeth and Ethan both looked to Brenna who only managed a quick nod. Elizabeth rose, allowing the doctor to take her place. She set her hands on Amanda's arms. "My dear, there's no need for you to stay through this. Go, get some fresh air."

Amanda hesitated with one last glance at Brenna, then at the doctor, before Elizabeth scooted her from the room. She didn't stop, instead making her way through the house until she stepped outside. The cool evening air hit her skin, drying up some of the perspiration that had accumulated on her face. She knew it didn't have as much to do with the heat of the bedroom as it did with the man tied up in the barn.

"How is Brenna doing?"

With a hand to her chest and a soft gasp, Amanda turned.

"I didn't mean to startle you."

"I'm a little on the edge of my nerves at the moment. Brenna is strong, and I believe doing well."

Ben grinned and leaned against the railing. "Guess it's tough to tell in situations like this."

"I'm grateful Ramsey and Eliza returned with the doctor when they did. Brenna's in good hands with him and Elizabeth." She shifted on her feet and gripped the nearest post. "Has he said anything else?"

Ben walked up the few steps to stand near her on the porch. "He will only speak with you. I told him that wasn't going to happen, but of course it's your choice."

She wanted to say no, preferring never to look at the man again, but strength pushed aside cowardice. "I would like to see him."

Ben nodded and held out a hand. Amanda was surprised by the gesture, but a deeper look at his expression told her she shouldn't be. She slipped her hand into his, stepped off the porch, and walked alongside him to the barn.

The scent of hay and livestock mingled with the cool air they brought in when Ben opened the barn doors. There in the corner, perched on a bale of hay someone had in generosity covered with a blanket, sat Stratton Cobb.

He stood. Colton pushed him back down. "Don't move again." Stratton held up his hands in a form of surrender and resettled himself on the hay.

"I knew you'd come to see me. You were always a quiet one, but I never took you for weak, and I'm glad to see I was right."

"You don't know anything about me." Amanda walked across the dusty and hay-strewn boards. "You killed my father."

"No." Stratton Cobb pointed his large, gloved hand at her. "No, I did not do that. I may be many things, but a murderer is not one of them."

From beside Amanda, Ben was able to look down slightly on Stratton. "If what you say is true, why have you been looking for her?"

Stratton ignored Ben, his focus intent on Amanda. "You're mistaken about me. I'm not here to kill you."

"Then why are you here?"

Colton asked the question, and Amanda watched Stratton, expecting him to answer as though the words had been her own. He stood now, holding up a hand to ward off action from one of the men. Amanda shook her head at them both. "Wait, let him answer the question first."

Stratton sighed and dared a step toward Amanda. "I'm here to help you."

STRATTON COBB WAS TALL, a decade older

than Ben, and strong. His dark eyes bore an arrogance Ben had seen too often in lawmen believing they were without judge, jury, or council. The image of one particular lawman from his past rose to the surface of his memories, and he quickly shook it away.

"Why don't I believe you, Mr. Cobb?"

Stratton turned away from Amanda for the first time and faced Ben. "I don't know you and you have no reason to trust me, especially after the stories I'm sure you've heard from our friend here."

"We're not friends." Amanda stepped around Ben, brushing his hand aside when he would have held her back. "I heard you the night my father died. I heard you in the store."

"I was there."

Amanda turned at the sound of voices coming from outside.

"That will be Henry and Pete coming in to sit with him. I'll keep them away until you're done." Colton walked to the open barn doors and handed his rifle to Ben on the way out.

16

HERE TO HELP HER? After admitting he was there when her father was killed? "Tell me, Mr. Cobb, why should I believe you when my better judgment tells me to let these men turn you over to the law—the real and honest law?"

"I'll have to start somewhere at the beginning in order for you to understand."

The loud smack of flesh connecting with flesh surprised her until she realized it was her palm that stung and Cobb's face now flushed red from her hand. Ben stepped in between them even as she moved back a few feet.

When she looked up, Cobb hadn't

moved, and Ben stood at an angle where he could watch the other man even as he studied her.

"Nothing you say will help me understand the role you've played in my father's death."

Cobb stroked the cheek she had assaulted. "I deserved it. But if it's the truth you're after, then you'll have to listen."

Amanda knew he was right—hated that she needed anything from this man— except the truth was all that mattered to her right now.

She steeled her back and crossed her arms over her chest, wishing she had thought to take a shawl from the house. "If you didn't kill my father, who did?" She stepped a few inches closer. "Who was with you in the store that night?"

"Baldwin Irving."

Amanda believed him, had even believed the banker guilty. Except the banker's involvement made no sense. She'd replayed the night over and over, considering every possible motive. She had convinced herself Irving's desire to see her jailed had been a show of strength for the town. Why would a wealthy banker want her father dead over a small mercantile?

She searched her memory for the words spoken that night. *I don't care what Kelly likes or doesn't. I own him, this store, and half this bloody town.* "We had nothing Mr. Irving could want. Our store was paid, free and clear, and my father bought the land without credit. I have the deeds to prove it."

"You think Irving cares? He does own the town. Your family was one of the few who managed on their own, paid their debts, and didn't have to go to Irving for loans. He hated your father."

Ben drew Cobb's attention away when he asked, "Then what was Irving doing there if he had no control? Why have her father killed?"

Cobb looked back to Amanda, his demeanor almost begging her to understand what he was about to tell her. "I've done a lot I'm not proud of, and plenty of dirty work Irving wouldn't do himself, but I never killed for him. I didn't know he was going to have those men kill anyone. He was looking for your deeds."

Ben said, "He had you and others to dirty their hands for him. Why was he there? Why go himself?"

"He didn't want anyone else to know." Cobb said to Amanda, "Except for the small cabin, your family never built on the land you own outside town."

Confused now, Amanda shook her head. "My father didn't want to live out there once my mother passed. He blamed himself for her weak heart and . . . Why does Mr. Irving want my land?"

"Gold, Miss Kelly. He didn't want your

land, he wanted your gold."

Amanda stared, flabbergasted and feeling like a fool. "Mr. Irving wanted to court me, and I deflected his advances. He wasn't as kind after that. My family was not indebted to him, which gave him no sway or control over me."

Ben held the rifle pointed to the floor rather than at Cobb, but Amanda knew how quickly he could raise a gun and fire when necessary. "How does he know there's gold on the land?"

"By chance. You were too young to remember the man who owned the land before your father. He died shortly after the money changed hands and willed everything he had left to the town, including a farfetched story about finding a gold nugget once. He searched and searched for years and never found another. It was a tale told to other men and more men over the years. No one believed him and thought the old man was a little crazy."

"Irving believed the story," Ben said in understanding.

Cobb nodded, sat back down on the hay bale, and rested his bound hands on his lap. "He believed it enough to send a few men to survey and assay the land to see what they could find. It was far enough away from town that they could do this without you or your father ever knowing."

"And they found gold." Bewildered and trying desperately not to believe the plausible explanation, Amanda wished for her own bale of hay on which to sit, but she couldn't bring herself to show any weakness.

"They discovered a new vein from the existing mine that extends onto your land. Irving wants an empire, and he needs your gold to get it."

Shouts and laughter from outside startled Amanda enough to step back and move toward the door. Ben remained close to Cobb. "It's Gabriel. When did he get . . . Oh, the baby!" Amanda didn't look back when she rushed from the barn and into the open air. Gabriel stood half distance from the house, sharing the news with Colton and the others.

Out of breath, Amanda reached Gabriel and his grin told her all she needed to know. "The baby is here? It's safe?"

He nodded and gave her a big, brotherly hug. "Isabelle saw right through me and insisted on being here. She's inside now with the children. A girl. They have a beautiful little girl."

17

Iron City, Dakota Territory
September 1866

FERGUS KELLY, WHAT HAVE you done?" Deirdre, his wife of ten years, spread her arms wide. "We can't possibly need all of this land."

"I'm not so sure about that." Fergus winked at his daughter, and Amanda returned the sentiment with a giggle. "It will be Amanda's one day, and the price was too good to pass for two hundred acres."

"Heavens, but you're a strange man, Fergus. My dear mother told me there'd be no end to surprises from you, and she was right." Deirdre draped an arm over

Amanda's shoulders and guided her back to the wagon. "Your pa has surely done it now."

When they were all loaded in the wagon, Amanda asked, "Pa, is this all ours?"

"It is, my girl, it's all ours." He motioned for her to join them on the seat in front, and once she was settled between her parents, her father tucked her under his arm and pointed in the distance. "We can have any life we want out here."

"Does this mean Mama's heart will be better?"

Fergus and Deirdre exchanged surprised glances. Amanda didn't understand everything she heard in the whispered conversations, and she knew better than to listen, but her father had sounded so worried on their journey west. Her mother always looked so pale.

"Your mother will do well here, don't you think?" Fergus asked. "We'll get her heart strong again. Why, she'll be stronger than us both soon!"

Amanda giggled and slipped one small hand into each of her parent's grasp. "She'll be strong as a horse!"

"Nay, ten horses!" Fergus added.

"Ten horses? Fergus, you do go on," Deirdre said, but her skin now had a rosy glow. Amanda agreed with her father—these rocky hills with their green forests would make her mother's heart better again.

Deirdre Kelly passed away quietly the following spring.

Amanda stood beside her father at the narrow grave, his hand clasped with hers. She understood death, knew her mother wasn't coming back. They moved out of the little cabin her father had built on the beautiful land and into the space above the store two weeks later. Her father's sadness may have dwindled, or Amanda thought it had. They visited the land and her mother's grave every spring, but Fergus Kelly never stepped inside the cabin again.

18

Hawk's Peak, Montana Territory
May 1884

AMANDA CHOKED BACK THE memories and held the sleeping baby, in awe over the miracle Brenna and Ethan had brought into the world. Of course, they had help, and thanks to Elizabeth and Doc Brody, the new addition had been born into her family without difficulty. The light fluff of red hair and look of the Gallaghers attested to the beautiful child's parentage.

Her attention left the little girl long enough to smile at the happy parents, who both looked exhausted. They sat close together on the bed, Brenna tucked beneath Ethan's arm, and the family all around. Isabelle didn't want to be left out and made it up the stairs with the help of her husband.

Isabelle settled into a chair by the bed, Gabriel at her side so they could be see the new baby. "I don't want to know how difficult it really was, Brenna, but I'll admit I'm anxious to hold my own child soon."

Brenna's smile brightened her tired eyes. "Oh, soon enough, and when you look into your son's—"

"Daughter's," Gabriel interjected, drawing laughs from the around the room.

"Daughter's eyes," Brenna grinned at her brother-in-law, "you'll only remember the joy."

The children were most in awe, and Catie declared herself the big sister of the most beautiful baby to ever be born. Amanda gently gave up the baby to Ethan's waiting arms now that everyone had a chance to admire and rock the new

Gallagher.

"Have you chosen a name?" she asked them. Everyone else in the room seemed to lean forward, eager to know as well.

Brenna and Ethan exchanged a soft and loving look before Brenna said, "Rebecca Victoria Gallagher."

Eliza smiled and walked to stand next to her brother where she took another peek at the child sleeping in his arms. "You've given this little girl two very proud names from two remarkable women. She does have a touch of mother in her, doesn't she, Ethan?"

Ethan nodded, and Brenna said, "I would haved loved to have known Victoria."

Though tired, Brenna smiled at her sister-in-law. "You never knew my mother, but she would have loved you all dearly." Brenna's eyes met Ramsey's as he joined his wife. "I should have spoken with you first about calling her Rebecca, but—"

"No, you shouldn't have. Knowing how much you loved our mother and how she loved you is enough." Ramsey bent and placed a kiss on his sister's cheek. "You've made me an uncle twice over—well, three now that we have Catie in the family—and I couldn't be more proud."

ELIZABETH SHOOED THEM ALL of out of the bedroom, claiming the mother and baby needed their rest. Another look at Ethan before she filed from the room told Amanda the happy father could probably use some sleep, too.

An hour later, she, Gabriel, and Isabelle were the only ones left in the parlor. The children went to bed soon after they had spent time with the baby. Jacob didn't fully understand what had happened, or who the small person in his parents' arms was, but his curiosity had him putting his nose close to hers, and he grinned when his new sister yawned.

Catie didn't want to leave baby Rebecca's side, but soon her drowsy eyes wouldn't remain open, so she was escorted to the nursery, and she fell asleep on the big bed with Jacob and Andrew.

Isabelle leaned into Gabriel and rested her hands on her belly. "I have to admit I'm even more excited now for our little one to arrive. I'm not sorry I missed the beginning part of tonight's activity. I'm not sure how I would have handled seeing firsthand what's in store for me."

Amanda held a smile and decided to keep the details of Brenna's labor to herself. No first-time mother should have to see or hear about it, though Amanda suspected Isabelle knew enough if she preferred to remain semi-ignorant. "It won't be much longer now, will it?"

"Another month yet," Isabelle said. "Though it may as well be sooner. I can barely get around these days. I was told the sickness would go away after the first few months, but mine returned almost as bad as in the beginning. Still, I can hardly wait."

Gabriel said to his wife, "The weeks will slip by quicker than you can imagine."

Isabelle lost her smile and gave her a husband a look which clearly said, *If you think it's so easy, you try it*. Amanda giggled, not knowing from where the sound came. She didn't think she had any more laughter in her tonight.

"The sun will be up in a few hours." Gabriel stood and helped his wife up from the sofa. "Are you retiring as well, Amanda?"

Amanda stared into the fire Gabriel had lit and shook her head. "I'm not as tired as I should be. I think I'll read for a bit."

Gabriel gave her the stern concerned look of a brother—or at least a look she believed an older brother would give—and asked, "You should rest, Amanda. I know there's a lot to settle, but it doesn't have to happen tonight. Cobb will still be here when the sun comes up."

How did they all read her so well? Was she so transparent? "I'm wound up, I won't deny it, and tonight is a time for celebration." Amanda wouldn't make a promise she didn't intend to keep. "I won't see him alone, if that's your concern."

"Gabriel told me of this Mr. Cobb," Isabelle said, leaning against her husband for support. "We all worry."

"I'm grateful, and again, I promise I won't see him alone."

Neither of them appeared to be satisfied with her vague response, and Amanda didn't doubt Gabriel would say something to Ethan and Ramsey and together they would stand beside her while she battled her own demons in search of the truth. And yet they had their own lives and concerns, and the last thing Ethan and Brenna needed right now was to worry about her and Cobb. As much as she wanted to lean on them all, she had to find a way to stand on her own.

They said their good-nights and Amanda walked to one of the bookshelves. Her long fingers skimmed volume after volume, but nothing piqued her interest. She found herself thinking about Stratton Cobb, and for the briefest of seconds wondered if they'd found him a warm place to sleep for the night.

Her body shuddered and she shook the thought from her mind. She didn't care what happened to him, and Amanda continued to tell herself that even as she reached for the shawl she'd left draped on a chair and walked outside. All was silent save the whisper of the wind and the gentle rustle of trees. Even the bunkhouse was dark, though Amanda knew at least two men would be awake, guarding Cobb.

She'd left the barn in a rush, thinking only of Brenna and the new baby, but now she wanted to speak with Cobb again, to learn more. He still hadn't explained why he'd come looking for her.

"Are you sure you want to go back in there?"

Amanda shouldn't have been surprised to hear Ben's voice or to find him standing in the darkness near the house. He was ever near these days, and she found his presence—knowing he was there if she needed him—to be a great comfort. "I honestly don't know."

He stepped from the shadows but did not climb the stairs. "How's the baby?"

The image of the little girl wrapped in the beautiful plaid blanket Brenna had brought from Scotland flitted through Amanda's mind and brought a smile to her lips. "She's perfect. Rebecca Victoria Gallagher. Ethan, I'm certain, will enjoy showing her off to everyone once they've had a chance to rest."

A need to be closer to Ben, to draw upon his strength, drew Amanda down the steps where she leaned against the wood railing. From her new vantage point, she was about eye level with Ben. He hadn't changed yet either and his presence held a blend of weariness and determination. She believed he wouldn't rest until she did, or at least until Stratton Cobb was no longer in the territory.

"We should both get some much-needed sleep."

Ben nodded and crossed his arms as he relaxed against one of the hitching posts. She watched him stare into the distance, but at what she couldn't tell. Beyond them lay the same land and outbuildings she'd come to recognize as part of the place she called home. Beyond those stood the mountain peaks, still packed with snow at the top. The moon's brilliant light brightened the dark-blue sky as stars twinkled.

Amanda spent many nights upon these steps, staring up at the sky and mountains.

She wondered what the world would look like from atop the highest peak, and wouldn't it be lovely if she could reach for those stars and feel the burn with her own fingertips, to touch such a wonder. "Fanciful thoughts" is what her mother used to call them, and Amanda spent more time of late than ever before filled with whimsical notions.

Ben broke through her thoughts when he said, "The rest of the men have been told about Cobb and why he's here. Ethan planned to tell them when the need for it arose, but no one expected him to show up unexpectedly."

"What a nuisance I've become. No, don't look at me like that. I know the family, you, and the others don't think of me as a botheration, but I can't help feeling like one. I'll never forget Nathan Hunter, or the pain and deaths he caused, not to mention Tyre Burton, that awful man's . . . lackey. When I arrived here in the middle of those nightmares, my troubles seemed ridiculous by comparison. They still do, and yet in here," she pounded a fist to her chest, "I live with the horror of my father's death every day. For a time, I thought the heartache would dull, but it's worse now that Cobb has arrived. He's brought that nightmare back and I can't close my eyes for fear of reliving it."

Amanda didn't know what to expect, but the tears welling in her eyes, or Ben's arms around her, were both swift and startling.

"It's all right to let go, Amanda." he whispered against her hair. "Heartache reminds us we're alive, but it doesn't last forever. You're allowed to grab hold of every moment of happiness you can find."

She tightened her arms around his waist, her face pressed against his shoulder. It wasn't proper, and Amanda Kelly had been raised to be a respectable lady. Except, at this moment, she no longer cared.

It wasn't clear who eased back first, or whether Ben caressed her cheek before her hand slid up and behind his neck. When their lips met, it didn't matter who kissed whom first because they both wanted—and needed—the coming together of flesh and soul. His mouth was gentle at first, almost hesitant. She heard the soft sigh escape her own lips, and her fingers moved upward to glide through his thick hair. The simple action broke down both of their defenses.

The kiss deepened. Ben became possessive and his passion and longing surprised and exhilarated her. Amanda couldn't remember who initiated the moment, but it was Ben who ended the connection.

Amanda slowly came back to reality and found herself still in Ben's arms, a smile on the lips which had only seconds before turned her attraction into a deep and undeniable desire.

"You can't know how much I want to finish what we've started tonight, but I can't—we can't."

"I know."

He pressed his forehead against hers, their breath mingled, and with one last gentle kiss on her sensitive lips, Ben stepped back.

19

AMANDA DIDN'T SEE COBB after she left
Ben's warm embrace and made her way
inside to her bedroom. Still fully clothed,
and uncertain if she could manage to
undress without fumbling, she sat on the
steamer trunk at the foot of the bed. She
knew she needed to sleep and bathe, and
it wouldn't be long before the sun crested
the mountains and set the valley aglow to
start the day anew.

She touched her fingers to her lips, the
memory of Ben's kiss potent. They'd held
each other beneath the moonlight for what
could have been forever, and Amanda
wished it didn't have to end. Every glance

he'd sent her way since she arrived, every time he went out of his way to help her, all made sense now, and she chided herself for believing her heart was unaffected.

The truth had revealed itself tonight. It hadn't been Cobb's arrival or the excitement of baby Rebecca's birth. Ben, and he alone, stirred her to the core, and she regretted the doubt and hesitancy she glimpsed in his eyes when they said good night. He did not doubt his feelings for her, that she could see. His uncertainy lay in whether or not her reciprocation was because she needed a release, an outlet for her suppressed emotions, or because she felt the same way about him as he did about her.

She did not blame him for wondering about her true feelings. Amanda held back the one part of her soul that would free her from the past and allow her to accept the deep and growing affection for Ben. Her heart pounded with the truth and she could no longer deny either of them the beauty of what could come from it. Only, Ben was right. His love for her was evident in every look, every action, but she had to come terms with her father's death. Before she could be free, truly free, she had to release the last vestige of hate from her heart.

Amanda looked around the spacious room and decided the bed would remain made and the wash bowl would suffice for a quick sponge bath. Elizabeth would have stayed awake much of the night, watching over the baby as the new parents slept. Catie would likely remain in bed and then be too excited about her new sister to spend much time downstairs. Amanda didn't expect to get any sleep before the sun began to peek through the windows.

Once she'd washed and changed her clothes, she made her way back downstairs. Her mind and body teetered on exhaustion, and she summoned the energy to set aside her worries long enough to prepare breakfast. It was with some surprise when she heard the footsteps on the steps by the kitchen door. The knob turned, and Amanda experienced a second of fear that Cobb had somehow escaped, but it was Eliza who stepped inside.

"Ramsey figured you'd be sleeping well into the day," Eliza said as she slipped off a long canvas duster to hang it on one of the pegs by the door.

"I couldn't possibly." Amanda brushed away a fallen strand of hair and smiled at Eliza. She wore one of her custom riding skirts, and Amanda found herself wondering if she could get a pair made for herself. "What are you doing awake? It's early even for you."

Eliza snatched a berry from the bowl Amanda had set out to make a blueberry pie later. "Ramsey and I slept for a couple of hours but that's all either of us could manage." Eliza leaned against the sink and relaxed her arms over her chest. Even in her casual work clothing and her hair in a long braid down her back, Eliza bore the striking good looks of the Gallaghers—piercing blue eyes set against clear skin and framed by dark hair, sometimes touched with gold from the sun. Eliza asked, "You haven't been to sleep, have you?"

Amanda straightened and for a moment ignored the bread dough she'd been kneading. "Would you like some tea?"

"I've already had two cups of coffee, but you go ahead." Eliza sat in one of the chairs at the table and waited for Amanda to sit across from her. "You should know Ramsey's out with Cobb right now."

Amanda stiffened. "It's barely three o'clock in the morning."

"It's too early to start work with the horses or to visit his new niece, and to

Ramsey's way of thinking, Stratton Cobb doesn't get to rest while you're losing sleep over him."

"You knew I would be awake?"

Eliza reached for another berry and took her time swallowing as she studied Amanda. "I know what I would do if I was in your situation, and it wouldn't be sleeping. Ramsey—well, all of us—want to see this matter with Cobb settled and him gone. Don't worry, we aren't going to rush you, but—"

"I don't feel rushed," Amanda said before Eliza could continue. "Though I should be the one out there right now." She looked to the window where darkness still fought to keep the morning at bay. "I want answers and damned be the time or anyone else's convenience." She stood and removed her white apron. "I'll return once I'm satisfied with what Cobb has to say."

Eliza grinned and rose from her chair. "I wondered when we'd see this Amanda again."

"What do you mean?"

"The Amanda Warren who journeyed across some of this country's most dangerous land, through Indian territory, and after all that, still had the gumption to become a part of this family." Eliza slipped an arm around Amanda's shoulders. "Come on. You're not doing this without me."

RAMSEY WASN'T ALONE WITH Cobb in the barn. Ben stood casually against one of the beams, focused on Cobb until Amanda and Eliza walked through the doors. The crisp night air hadn't penetrated through Amanda's clothing, which she attributed that to her indignation. Their eyes met. The kiss, the longing for him, bubbled to the surface of her thoughts, and it was only with a gentle nudge from Eliza that she turned her attention away from Ben.

Ramsey intercepted Amanda and Eliza

before they made it halfway to Cobb.

"Has he said anything more?" Amanda asked in a whisper.

Ramsey rolled his shoulders to ease his tense muscles and shook his head. "He still insists on speaking with you. We haven't been able to persuade him to tell us anything we haven't already figured out."

Amanda nodded and when Ramsey stepped to the side, she closed the distance between her and Cobb. Ben had moved when she did and now stood only a few feet away. She didn't dare spare him a glance, not if she was going to hold onto the so-called gumption Eliza claimed Amanda possessed.

"My father . . . Did you know Mr. Irving was going to have him killed? Did you suspect?"

"I would have warned him, warned you," Cobb said. "I'd say you should believe me on that score, but I know I no longer have the right to ask for your trust."

"No, you don't. I imagine Mr. Irving would rather I disappear, and I did for a time. What I don't understand is why you've come after me. I wasn't coming back." The truth of those words hit Amanda with tremendous force. She had land where her parents were buried, and a home if she wanted it, but she'd found her place here.

Cobb looked to Ben who after a few seconds nodded once, and then he stood, his bound hands hanging down in front of him. "You own the big stretch of land outside Iron City, which means you own the gold in the earth. As long as you're alive, Irving can't claim right to any of it."

"You mean he can try to claim the rights if she wasn't alive?" Eliza asked, stepping forward.

"A man like Baldwin Irving will do whatever he has to in order to get what he wants, and he wants your land, Miss Kelly.

If he can't buy it from you, he'll find less-than-legal means to take it."

Ramsey said, "You mean, he'll kill her and falsify a will? That's not as easy to do as some men think. No one would believe it."

"No," Cobb said, "But he's done it before, and she doesn't have any family to speak of. Not too many people would overthink such a will."

Realization hit Amanda and she'd never felt more the fool. "It wasn't my father's deed or will he wanted, but any will I might have drawn up. To know what I had planned before he tried to . . . kill me. Why didn't he explain about the gold? I know we turned him down before, but if he came to me, explained—"

"He wants everything, and if the gold vein goes as deep as they suspect, it runs not far from where your parents are buried." Cobb appeared to study her. "You wouldn't have sold everything."

Amanda shook her head, understanding how desperate Irving must truly be to go to all this trouble. "No, I wouldn't have disturbed my parents in such a way or allowed him to, either."

"Miss Kelly—"

"I haven't been Miss Kelly for some time now." Amanda stepped closer to Cobb, prompting all three of her companions to close their distance a little as well. "You still haven't said why you came here, and as you claim, to warn me. Why now?"

Cobb's voice was barely a whisper when he said, "I've done enough wrong by you and your family. If I'm going to my grave, it's not going to be without trying to right my sins."

"You believe you're now forgiven for what happened to my father? You may not have pulled the trigger or hired Barker, but you played your part."

Cobb had nothing to say, and Amanda

didn't know what she expected him to do. Confess and prove right every vile thing she'd thought about him? She turned away and walked toward the door before she stopped.

Without looking at him, she asked, "Does he know where I am?"

"Not yet, but he will."

"When are you supposed to tell him?"

The gasp which escaped Amanda's lips was involuntary. She turned and stared at Ramsey. "What do you mean?"

Ramsey nodded toward Cobb. "If I was in his position, and assuming I spoke the truth, I'd do my best to misdirect Irving, but that doesn't mean I wouldn't still work for the man."

Amanda returned to the spot she'd vacated in front of Cobb. This time Ben stood within a foot of her. "Is that true?" she asked Cobb.

"It is."

"Where does he think she is now?" Eliza

asked.

"On her way to Oregon." Cobb lowered himself down onto the hay bale.

"You better be telling the truth." Ben's voice was soft, yet firm, and might not have carried to the others had they not been intent on the conversation.

The barn doors swung open and there stood Gabriel and Ethan. Ethan said, "Looks like we're missing all the fun."

Ethan and Gabriel took in the scene, assessing each individual before they moved forward in tandem to where Eliza stood. Alone they could make a person cautious. Together, they were fierce and intimidating.

Amanda knew each of them possessed a heart as pure and kind as a human could have, but that didn't stop the momentary hitch of her breath when Ethan walked toward her. Despite the weariness he must feel, the lines around his eyes softened when he faced her. "Brenna asked for you.

She's worried herself so much she won't rest until she knows you're all right. Would you mind going to her?"

"Of course not." Amanda glanced once more at Cobb before leaving the barn. The impact of the cool, morning air washed over her face and cooled her rising temper.

"Give yourself a minute." Ben walked beside her, and she hadn't heard him approach from behind. "It's okay to take a little time to calm down before you go inside."

Amanda released a staggering breath and stopped. The first vestige of morning light glowed beyond the mountain range, and soon the stars would succumb to sleep when the sun dismissed them. She'd been in the barn longer than she'd realized.

"Do you believe him, Ben? What he's told us, about misdirecting Irving and trying to protect me, goes against everything I believe him guilty of."

"I do believe him." Ben wondered if she

realized how much she rev
look or the slightest move
body. "I trusted a lawman o
time ago, and I lost what I lo
because he betrayed my family. Fo
time I looked at all men like him the s
never truly believing what they said—o
them as people—but over time, I learne
to trust my instincts when it came to
measuring the honesty of a man's words."

Ben unfolded her arms and held her
hands, her smooth skin belying the
strength he felt beneath. "Tell me what
you are thinking."

Her golden hair reflected the light from
the waning moon, and when she met his
eyes, he knew he'd wait a lifetime for her.

"If what he says is true, then there's an
opportunity, is there not?"

"What do you mean?"

"We give him what he wants," Amanda
said without hesitation.

ealed with one
ment of her
ce, a long
ed most
a long
ame,
in

ME YOU don't mean what I—

Yes, I do." Amanda started back for the barn, no doubt intent on sharing her plan with the others.

"Wait, Amanda, just wait." Ben ran a hand through his hair because it was a better choice than shaking sense into her. "I can't decide if I'd rather have the frightened and uncertain you back instead of . . . this is a foolhardy idea and you know it."

"Am I wrong?"

"No, damn it." Ben took a deep breath. "I'm sorry. Why, Amanda? You don't have to prove anything, and what you're talking about is dangerous."

"I have no intention of dying, Ben Stuart. The law won't allow me to point a finger and claim Baldwin Irving killed my father or had me unjustly arrested. Sheriff Cobb's word isn't enough without evidence. Besides, Irving is too wealthy, and a man like him will find a way to ensure I never say a word against him."

Ben didn't quite know what to make of the woman before him. He knew she was strong, able, and willing to fight for her life, for good, but he didn't imagine for a moment she would sacrifice her life for the truth. "You haven't looked evil head-on, not knowing if the next breath you take could be your last."

"And you have?"

"Yes!" Ben hated the anger swelling within him, anger he believed existed only in his past.

"Tell me I'm wrong, Ben." She reached

for his hands again and pulled him closer to her. "Tell me nothing will come of it, that if I do this, I'll lose everything. Tell me, and I won't speak of it again. I'll go into the house, hold the beautiful new baby in my arms, and tell Ethan I don't want to speak with or see Stratton Cobb ever again."

He released her hands, but only so he could slide his up her arms and draw her nearer. His lips met hers in a storm of passion, the need to release his furious fear before he said the words he might one day regret. The need, though it would never be gone, had for the moment subsided. When he eased back, her eyes were closed and her lips swollen and rosy from the kiss.

"You're not wrong." He rested his forehead against hers, waiting for their racing hearts to calm.

"Everything all right here?"

Ben and Amanda pulled away and

turned at the sound of the voice. They'd been too caught up in each other to have heard their approach. Ethan and Eliza stood close enough for Ben to see the concern on Ethan's face and the curious smile on Eliza's.

"Yes, I'm going in to see Brenna and the baby now." Amanda looked at Ethan and said, "I know how much you care, but I'm going to ask you not to play the big brother right now, please." She turned and walked the rest of the way to the house.

Eliza gave Ben a parting, "It's about time," as she followed Amanda.

"We heard shouting," Ethan said. "Should I be worried?"

"Not about me or how I feel." Ethan stood a few inches taller, but Ben managed to meet his scrutinizing stare. "You've known for a long time how I feel about her."

It wasn't a question and Ethan didn't deny it. "We all know, and I couldn't be happier for two people I love if it's what you both want, but I'm not going to pretend I don't worry about her. What was the argument about?"

"Cobb, Irving, Amanda's foolishness." Ben recounted the conversation he had with Amanda. When he'd finished, Ethan's anger equaled his own, though he'd had time to calm down some.

"I swear, we're a refuge for stubborn women," Ethan said and kneaded the back of his neck. "In a lot of ways she reminds me of Eliza, and that scares the hell out of me."

If Ben wasn't mistaken, Ethan looked ready to smile. "You wouldn't want them any other way, would you?"

"No, but there are times." Ethan shifted his gaze to look out over the land they'd fought to keep and a life they'd struggled to build. "She has the right to do this, Ben."

"I know, and if it were anyone else but

her . . ."

Ethan slapped Ben's back in a brotherly fashion. "I know the feeling."

AMANDA WATCHED FROM THE doorway of Brenna's bedroom as mother and daughter bonded. Brenna's lyrical Highland accent sounded stronger as she sang a soft lullaby in the beautiful Gaelic she slipped into sometimes. Amanda tried to learn a few of the words, but her tongue always felt like it twisted during her attempts to sound like Brenna.

"She'll have her papa terrified when it comes time for courting."

Brenna looked up, her smile wide and her brilliant green eyes aglow. "Don't say such a thing to Ethan, though you're right. Come, say hello."

Amanda moved to the bedside and sat down. Brenna transferred the baby into her arms. "You're a natural with her, and you'll make a lovely mother someday."

"How anyone could look upon such a face and not love her, I wouldn't understand it. What were you singing?"

"An old Gaelic lullaby my mother sang to me as a child."

"It's as lovely as your new daughter." Amanda traced a finger over the baby's soft cheek. "Ethan said you wanted to see me, and if it was only to say hello again to this little one, then I'm glad you've called."

The baby held fast to Amanda's finger as she gently rocked her in her arms. "I did have a motive in mind when I asked to see you. I don't want to give you more to think on than you already have, but I'd—Ethan and I—would like to ask if you'd be Rebecca's godmother."

Tears filled Amanda's eyes before she could fully process what had been asked of her. "What about Eliza or Isabelle? They're family."

"Don't upset a new mother. Haven't you been told? We're wildly unpredictable with our emotions." Brenna smile softened. "You are as much family as they are. Besides, Eliza is already spoken for as Jacob's godmother, and we spoke with Gabriel and Isabelle about this. At the rate we're going, there will be plenty of children to share, and there is no one Ethan and I would rather have fill this role than you. Please tell me you'll accept."

Joyful tears fell down Amanda's smiling face. "Of course I accept."

Ethan, who had quietly entered the room, met his wife's eyes, his grin matching her own. He watched the woman who was now every bit a part of their child's life as she was theirs, and he worried for her as much as he ever did Eliza. Had anyone told him his life would be filled with so many remarkable women of courage, he wouldn't have believed them.

He thought of what Ben had told him of Amanda's plans—her wishes—and he knew as sure as he knew his own sister, that he and the others would stand by Amanda's side whatever her choice. Ethan knew her journey wouldn't end until she'd found justice, in every way the Gallaghers had finally found theirs.

21

BEN MANAGED A FEW hours of sleep before he returned to the barn where Stratton Cobb had been provided with a cot and a few blankets. No one trusted him in the house, but neither would they be able to continue to keep him confined without notifying the Deputy U.S. Marshal.

Gabriel brushed his horse as Cobb slept. Ben leaned against the stall where the gelding was tied and nodded toward Cobb. "How long has he been out?"

"A few hours." Gabriel didn't stop the slow strokes of the brush when he asked, "When was the last time you slept a night through?"

"Probably the last time any of us did." Ben studied their visitor, his hands now unbound. "He's telling the truth, Gabriel."

Whether Gabriel agreed or not, he didn't say. Ben learned a long time ago that this particular Gallagher may be the charming rogue who was quick to smile and make friends, but he could also be as guarded as his siblings. He didn't have Ethan's temper or Eliza's cool regard when she scrutinized a person, but that only made him more unpredictable.

Gabriel did surprise him when he said, "You could be right. Do you think it's worth the risk, this plan of Amanda's?"

Ben should not have been surprised Gabriel had been told. "Hell, no. Except, it's what she wants."

"So you're going to keep quiet about it?"

Ben found himself shaking his head without thought or guidance. "Amanda and I . . . we don't . . . I mean she's still learning to trust everyone. Not that she didn't before, but this is different. When a person holds onto a troubled past for so long, keeping it to herself, it's diffcult to share. Once you do open yourself up, it's too hard to pull back and hide your feelings again."

The expression on Gabriel's face brought a chuckle from Ben. He glanced at Cobb to make sure he hadn't woken the man. Though, he wouldn't be surprised if Cobb was already awake.

Gabriel said, "Ben, I had no idea you were such a philosopher. And I don't think I've ever heard you say so many words at one time. You're usually as taciturn as my brother."

Ben managed a grin, though his thoughts remained cloudy. He sensed a storm coming, for Amanda and for him. He walked to Cobb and stood next to the cot. "Since you're awake, why don't you turn around and answer a question."

Cobb shifted his tall frame and dropped

his legs over the side of the cot. He waited for Ben to speak.

"You claim you aren't here to hurt her, so I'm going to ask you, will you do whatever it takes to help save her?"

Ben waited. He didn't expect an immediate answer, and while he could fault Cobb for not knowing if he was willing to stand on the side of justice, he couldn't blame him for choosing an honest response.

"No, not whatever it takes," Cobb said as he rose to his feet. "I came here to warn her, nothing more."

"You won't put her in harm's way, though," Gabriel said.

"No, I won't." Cobb held out his bound hands to Ben. "I'm not blind to what Irving has done or my part in it. I owe her at least my word that I won't harm her. This may be his land," Cobb said, nodding to Gabriel as he looked at Ben, "but she's yours. Send for the marshal and see me gone forever, or trust me because I'm your only link to Irving."

In Ben's mind, his link to Irving was why he shouldn't be trusted. He glanced at Cobb's wrist, the rope unfrayed. The man hadn't attempted to rid himself of the ties. Either he wasn't a fool or he meant what he said about helping Amanda. Either way, Ben would trust him, because Amanda needed him to, whether she realized it or not. He pulled a long blade from the leather sheath at his side and sliced through the ropes.

Cobb massaged his wrists where the rope had left them chafed. "What now?"

Gabriel stepped in front of Cobb, his height giving him an extra two inches over the other man. It wasn't much, but it was enough to make Cobb step back a foot. "You wire your boss and tell him you've found Amanda Kelly. Ask for instructions."

Cobb looked between the two men, his

stance confident but his eyes hesitant. "I already have my orders." He massaged his hands again, and his next words were spoken casually. "He's already told people she's dead."

AMANDA AWAKENED THE next morning with firm resolve to be rid of both Cobb and Irving. She'd not returned to the barn after spending time with Brenna and the baby. She needed to think, to plan, and she couldn't do either without sleep.

She made her way downstairs, feeling more herself after a few hours of rest, and was surprised to find Brenna at the table with Rebecca in her arms. Elizabeth sat across the table enjoying a cup of tea. Amanda heard the story of how Elizabeth came to be at Hawk's Peak after living in a small town a few days' ride north of Briarwood. Brenna said the adventurous journey to find her grandmother had been when she fell in love with Ethan.

"Should you be out of bed?" Amanda asked as she walked into the kitchen. Both women looked up, smiles on their faces.

"I feel wonderful." Brenna smoothed her hand over the baby's downy hair. "I promised Ethan not to overdo and to rest most of the day, but I needed to get out of bed."

Elizabeth said, "She's trying to convince me she's well enough to go for a walk."

"Only by the garden. I could do with the exercise."

Amanda tied a clean white apron around her waist and shook her head at Brenna. "You just had a baby." At Brenna's smirk and raised brow, Amanda said, "Of course you know this, but Brenna . . . you just had a baby."

"My father once told me that my mother woke up the day after she gave birth and went about her normal routine as though nothing extraordinary had happened." Brenna pressed a light kiss to her lips and transferred it to the baby's mouth. "A few minutes by the gardens won't hurt. One of you could walk with me."

Amanda looked to Elizabeth for help, but Brenna's grandmother raised her hands in defeat. "Don't let Ethan see you."

The Gallagher in question was busy listening to Gabriel explain what had transpired between him, Ben, and Cobb. He wanted to strangle them both, and he couldn't decide which of them would go first.

"You let him go alone?"

"No, Ben is staying close to him."

"Does Ben have any idea how angry Amanda is going to be? Not one woman on this ranch takes kindly to having their decisions made for them, and this is taking a big choice away from Amanda."

"Ben gets it, which is why he insisted he be the one to go with Cobb. Once Cobb sends the telegram, he'll get a room at the boardinghouse and wait."

Ethan rubbed a hand over his face, trying to wipe away some of the tiredness and frustration he currently felt. "I'll go and explain to Amanda. How is Isabelle?"

"As sweet as ever, except when she remembers I'm the one who put her in her current condition." Gabriel grinned like a man who would soon become a father. Ethan knew the feeling well. "Catie's at our house with her, though she's torn between helping Isabelle and spending time with the new baby."

"That girl is already the best big sister any kid could ask for." Ethan watched one of the ranch hands head toward the west pastures where he would spend a few hours checking the fences. "Have you thought about moving back into the main house until the baby is born?"

Gabriel nodded. "Isabelle and I have talked about it. She worries about imposing, especially when the baby may not come for another month. Eliza and Amanda have worked out a schedule to help Isabelle. My wife tells them it's unnecessary since she sleeps half the day, but they insisted."

"Let's be grateful there's only one more in this condition right now." Ethan managed a laugh, but Gabriel wasn't fooled.

"You're exhausted, Ethan. You have a new baby, a wife who needs you, and—"

"And a ranch to run."

"I've told Colton to handle some of the foreman duties while Ben is occupied with Cobb. Ramsey is handling—"

The scream wrenched through the air, a high-pitched and frightening cry that sent both men into a run.

22

BEN WALKED INTO THE telegraph office with Stratton Cobb, said hello to Orin Lloyd who stood behind the counter, and waited. "How's your family, Orin?"

"Oh, they're fine, thanks." Orin handed a piece of paper and pencil to Cobb and told him to write what he wanted on the telegram. Then he turned back to Ben. "Heard tell from Doc Brody there's a new baby at the ranch. Please pass along my congratulations to Ethan and his lovely wife."

"I will." Ben smiled, though he kept a close watch on what Cobb wrote. Cobb made no effort to hide the few scrawled lines before he passed the paper back to the telegraph operator.

Orin said to Cobb, "I'll get this sent right out."

"Appreciate it," Cobb said and paid before he exited the building.

Ben watched Cobb tip his hat at a passing lady and her son before he stepped off the board walk and continued down the street. Ben handed a letter to be posted and a few seconds later stepped outside.

As a young man, Ben learned trust was a fickle thing. Before he came to Hawk's Peak, trust had been a foreign experience for him. Since his arrival almost a decade ago, he'd slowly allowed himself to believe people were inherently good. He had his adoptive family to thank for his shift in thinking, but their kindness didn't mean he trusted everyone he met. Some he could read, a few he couldn't. When it came to Stratton Cobb, he couldn't decide if the man would be honorable in the end or if he proved Amanda right.

Erring toward doubt and caution for Amanda's sake, Ben crossed the street and walked toward the general store. He hadn't been a frequent visitor to the saloon since a month after his arrival in Briarwood, and his presence would have been noticed.

"Is that you, Ben Stuart?"

He turned and offered a smile to Loren's wife. "It is." He stepped out of the sun, closer to Joanna and the front door. "Pretty day out."

She nodded and wiped her hands on her practical white apron. "Sure is. Weren't you just in town the other day?"

Ben chuckled. "I can't seem to get enough of your pretty smile. If I didn't have competition in Loren, I'd whisk you away into the sunset."

Joanna swatted one of her hands at Ben and clucked her tongue. "I could be your grandmother, young man."

"I do believe you're about to break my heart, Mrs. Baker."

She played along, smoothed back her graying hair. "If only you'd been so lucky, Ben Stuart."

They enjoyed another laugh at their teasing. "Is Loren about? I haven't seen him much lately."

Ben wished he hadn't asked when he saw the light flutter from Joanna's eyes.

"He hasn't been himself lately. Doc Brody tells him he has to rest, but you know Loren. Stubborn as a mule. I sent him back to bed an hour ago. The doc says not to worry about Loren's gruffness and just keep telling him to take it easy."

"Well, if anyone can, it's you."

Joanna waved and said hello to a passing couple Ben didn't recognize. She hadn't called them by name, so he guessed they weren't locals. The Bakers tended to know most people who came through

Briarwood since they were the only store in town.

Ben kept an eye on the saloon's entrance when he asked Joanna. "Any new folks in town recently?"

Joanna pursed her lips and after a few seconds, nodded. "Well, those nice folks you just saw. I did meet a couple of friendly young men who just started working for that small farm of Langton Hughes. And there was a family of four who stopped through yesterday. I don't reckon they're still here, said they were visiting a sister before they moved on for Oregon. Can you imagine? Oregon! All the way from Georgia."

Ben listened as Joanna asked if he'd heard about the fancy new buggy Mr. Simmons, the editor of the newspaper, ordered. He shook his head, but he was focused on the saloon, not the storekeeper's wife. The shouts came first, followed in a few seconds by a gunshot.

Ben pushed Joanna back into the store. "Get behind the counter, and don't come outside until I tell you it's safe."

He knew she was frightened, but Ben didn't have time to comfort her. He ran to the saloon, pushed through the swinging doors, and was backed into the wall. Two brawling men didn't seem to care where they were or who they pushed into during their fight. Ben shoved them away and received a fist to his jaw for the effort before the original pair went back to their fighting.

The town needed a damn sheriff, he thought, before he grabbed one of the men from behind by his shoulders and swung him around, causing him to land back first on the wood floor.

"Millie! Where's your brother?"

Millie, the saloon owner's sister, said, "Fool got himself locked up in Bozeman for fighting with the sheriff's cousin."

The irony wasn't lost on Ben. He held a

hand against the man who remained standing. "Unless you want Millie here to put a bullet in your sorry hide, you'd best get out of here before I haul you off to the jail."

Ben was known in town and in the surrounding area as a longtime employee of the Gallaghers and the foreman of Hawk's Peak. Most folks knew messing with one of the Gallaghers' people was the same as going against them. Ben recognized the man as a former ranch hand for Nathan Hunter's spread. Most of the old man's employees had scattered after he died, and a few had found work on smaller ranches or farms in the area.

The young man, in his early twenties, pushed away from Ben and wiped a sleeve across his bloody mouth. "You self-righteous son of a bitch." He took another swing at Ben, only to be stopped this time by someone much taller and bigger than him.

Ben might have been amused by Cobb's interference if he didn't have to deal with the current problem at hand. "I don't know your name, and I don't care, but if you don't want to spend the night on a hard cot in a small cell, you'll get out of here and cool off before your friend wakes up."

"Name's Roy James. You and those Gallaghers think you're all better than the rest of us. Well, you ain't!" Roy spat on the floor and sneered at Ben.

Millie yelled, "You're going to clean that up, Roy."

"Shut up, Millie."

Ben grabbed Roy by the front of his shirt. He stood a few inches taller than the skinnier man who wasn't big enough to have started a fight in the first place. "James. Any relation to Bradford?"

Roy's eyes widened and he tried to pull away. Ben released him. Roy now realized they'd become the center of everyone's attention.

"Bradford was my cousin. That dumb shit Ethan Gallagher thought he was better than him, just like you do. Bradford didn't do nothing wrong!"

Ben didn't provoke easily and he didn't consider violence a ready answer when the other person was a fool. For Roy, he'd consider making an exception. Ben stepped closer, lowering his voice to a whisper so others couldn't hear. "Your cousin kidnapped a woman, intent on raping her. He deserved what he got." Ben stepped back and said louder, "Now get out of here."

Roy swiped his hat from the floor, and with eyes madder than a rabid wolf, stomped out of the saloon. The remaining customers quickly lost interest and went back to their drinking and card games.

Millie nodded her head in thanks and walked off, grumbling about stupid men. The man—more a kid—Ben had felled, moaned, and Ben reached down to help him up. A few more years and the strapping youth would be as big as Ethan.

"What's your name, kid?"

"Levi Gibbs, sir." Levi rubbed his sore jaw and looked around. "He's gone?"

"He's gone," Cobb said from behind Ben.

Ben ignored Cobb and handed Levi his hat. "Whatever the fight was about, wasn't worth it. He was giving you a pretty good row, but with your size, you could have really hurt him. I don't imagine you want to end up in jail, which could have happened if he hadn't walked out of here."

"No, sir. But, sir, he insulted my sister. I couldn't let that go unanswered for."

Ben studied the young man carefully. He couldn't be more than eighteen. "Gibbs? Your father Julius?"

Levi nodded. "Yes, sir."

Ben knew Julius Gibbs had been in a riding accident this past winter and broken his leg. Julius was a builder by trade, and there wasn't a lot of that going on in Briarwood at the moment. "Are you employed, Levi?"

"No, sir, not regular-like. No places big enough around these parts taking on new help."

"Do you think you can stay out of trouble?"

Levi hadn't caught on to where the conversation was going, but he nodded.

"There's one place big enough. Show up tomorrow, sunrise, at Hawk's Peak. Don't be late."

Levi's brown eyes opened wide, his mouth agape in surprise. "You mean it, Mr. Stuart?"

Ben nodded and pointed toward the door. "I don't want to ever hear about you being in this saloon again, Levi, at least not until you're older."

The surprise on Levi's face remained, but added to it was a big smile. "Yes, sir,

Mr. Stuart. I won't let you down. Thank you, sir!" Levi stumbled a little over his long legs in his rush to leave the saloon.

"You thought it was me."

Ben closed his eyes, hoped for patience, and turned to face Cobb. "Yes, I did."

Cobb leaned against the bar and motioned for Millie to refill his glass. "You're not stupid, I'll give you that. You ever been a lawman?"

Ben ignored the question, asking one of his own. "Do you always drink so much?"

Cobb raised a brow and downed the shot of whatever Millie had poured him. "No." He turned the glass over, placed a coin on the counter, and followed Ben outside. "I can't decide if I like you or not, Ben. You don't mind if I call you Ben, do you?"

"I do, but I doubt that's going to stop you." Ben continued to lead the way toward the livery. "And I don't care if you like me or not."

Cobb's voice lost the levity when he said, "I meant what I said about not wanting to see Amanda—Miss Warren—come to harm."

Frustrated and losing patience, Ben stopped walking and faced Cobb. He wanted to be back at the ranch, watching over Amanda, tending to the herd, and drawing plans for the new cabin he planned to build. He volunteered for this task because if anyone was going to accept the blame for taking control over the situation, he'd rather it be him.

"That's one truth I happen to believe." Ben continued on until he reached his horse. "I believe Irving pays you enough so you can afford a room at the boardinghouse."

"And here I thought you were going to stay in town and make sure I don't get into any trouble."

Ben swung up on his gelding and looked down at Cobb. "What makes you think I'm leaving?"

23

ETHAN REACHED THE HIGH pasture first and shouted for someone to run into town and get the doctor. He dismounted by the fallen horse, and a second later Gabriel knelt beside him.

"Is he alive?"

Ethan held his hand above Jake's mouth. "He's breathing, but not well."

Gabriel untied Jake's neckerchief and used it to staunch the bleeding. "This isn't a bullet wound, Ethan."

"Neither is this." Ethan gently tilted Jake's head to reveal a long, narrow gash on the back of his head. He pulled a rag from his pocket and pressed it against the wound.

They turned to find Ramsey and Colton racing toward them. They slowed their mounts to a stop a dozen feet away, and Colton dismounted. He hurried to Jake's side and asked, "Is he going to make it?"

Ethan nodded. "I think so, but he's lost a bit of blood. We can't move him without the wagon."

Ramsey turned his horse around and called over his shoulder, "We'll get the wagon out here!"

Colton studied the ground around Jake's body, walking in a wide circle before stopping next to Gabriel. "There was only one man."

"Can you find his trail?" Ethan asked.

Colton nodded and swung back on his horse as though there was no space between the ground and the saddle. "I'll find it."

Ethan didn't know what Colton had seen, and he'd learned long ago not to question the man after he'd proven he could track just about anything or anyone through the wilderness. He watched Colton disappear over a rise, heading west.

Gabriel managed to keep Jake from losing more blood through what they suspected was a large knife wound. The bleeding on the back of Jake's head had ceased for now. Jake had been checking on a section of the mountain stream that flowed through the Gallaghers' land. Spring runoff often brought with it debris and had to be cleared on occasion and watched closely to make sure it didn't dam up.

"He shouldn't have been out here alone."

Gabriel looked at his brother. "We all come out here alone, Ethan. You know it's not anyone's fault."

He did know, or at least the rational part of his mind did. Except no matter how often his brother, sister, wife, or anyone else told him something on the ranch wasn't his fault, they were wrong. Everything and everyone, from the moment they stepped foot onto Hawk's Peak, was his responsibility.

Ten minutes later, Ethan heard the men approach. They tended not to run the horses when they pulled a wagon, especially over the uneven pastures, but in this case, Ethan was glad they did.

Ramsey dismounted, and with the help of two other ranch hands, loaded Jake's unconscious body into the back. They'd brought blankets with them, and Ethan could only hope the man would live long enough for the doctor to patch him up.

Ethan, Gabriel, and Ramsey remained behind, Gabriel telling the men they'd follow in a minute. Ramsey glanced between the two brothers. "It's Hunter and Tyre all over again, isn't it? We thought this kind of madness was over."

Ethan wiped at the smeared blood on his hands and recalled the madness to which Ramsey referred. Hunter had been an enemy they could see, one they knew how to fight, but in the end, a greater enemy in Tyre Burton had emerged. Tyre, Nathan Hunter's personal gunfighter, had nearly taken Eliza from them. Knowing he was buried six feet deep didn't erase the sudden shock of fear that coursed through Ethan as he remembered almost losing his sister. "Are you suggesting that even though we've been worried about Cobb, someone else might be a greater danger?"

Ramsey nodded. "It's possible Irving is more dangerous than we expected—more determined than Amanda realizes—and he sent someone else."

"And Jake happened upon him," Gabriel added.

"Maybe."

Ethan considered this new scenario and wanted to be careful how they approached it. "If Amanda suspects any of this is because of her, she'll leave. I know she will, and she won't tell us she's going, not if she thinks anyone is any real danger."

"This isn't her fault."

"I know, Gabe, but she'll feel responsible." Ethan grabbed his stallion's reins and climbed into the saddle. "I want Cobb back here now. If Irving wants to hurt one of our own, then it's time we take this fight to him."

BEN WOKE AND HELD his pistol steady in front of him, pointing at the shadow moving toward him. He released the lever on his gun and lowered his hand. "What are you doing here?"

Ethan stepped from the shadows. "Glad to see your reflexes are working. Where's Cobb?"

"In the boardinghouse." Ben rose from his makeshift bed on the hay. "How you'd know I was here?"

"A good guess." Ethan stood beneath the entrance to Otis Lincoln's livery and stared out at the dark street. "Anything happen since Cobb sent the telegram?"

"No, it's been quiet. A fight at the saloon, and Doc Brody left this afternoon, but I didn't see where he headed."

"To the ranch." Ethan turned to Ben. "Jake was hurt."

Ben swore. "Is he going to be all right?"

"He's strong, and the doc said he was lucky. I want to speak with Cobb."

"It wasn't Cobb, Ethan. As much as none of us like him, he hasn't gone anywhere."

"I don't think it was Cobb, but I'd bet this has something to do with Irving. Ramsey believes Irving could have sent someone else when he didn't hear back from the good sheriff, someone who won't hesitate to get rid of Amanda."

He'll have to get through me first, Ben thought. "Does Amanda know?"

Ethan shook his head. "The doc treated Jake in the bunkhouse, but she'll have to be told."

"I'd rather be the one to tell her, if you don't mind."

"I figured you would."

"Did the person leave a trail?"

Ethan nodded. "Colton followed it for a few miles. The rider's tracks joined up with what Colton said looked like a small herd of cattle and three wranglers. When he found the herd, the men told him an injured rider had joined them until they crossed the river, then he rode south."

"The man knew what he was doing."

"Jake must have surprised him out there. At least he didn't have a chance to get to Amanda." Ethan looked back at Ben.

Ben didn't want to think about what would have happened. "Irving is getting desperate. I'd like to know why." He stepped outside, the light of the moon enough to illuminate the quiet town and empty street. Light in a few windows above businesses cast a glow in the darkness, reminding Ben that life, as normal and uneventful as it could be, was exactly what he wanted. "There's a kid coming out to the ranch tomorrow. I thought we could give him a try to fill Tom Jr.'s place now that he's gone off to college in Denver."

Ethan remained by the livery doors, his tall frame braced against the wood. "Who's the kid?"

"Levi Gibbs."

"Julius Gibbs' boy?"

"That's him. Pulled him out of the fight I mentioned earlier. His father's still laid up."

Ethan turned away from the street to look at Ben. "I'd heard. Gabe approached him about helping to build the new stables, but this was back when he couldn't move around well enough. We approached him a couple months back, offered to buy up some of his land. Thought it might help out, but he won't part with it. I haven't seen Levi since the family first moved to the area. You think he can do the job?"

Ben grinned. "He'll give you and Gabe a good run." He sobered when his thoughts shifted back to what Ethan had told him earlier. "How bad off is Jake?"

"He'll be laid up for a few weeks. It was bad. We weren't sure he'd make it. Someone stuck him with a knife—a big one—and left a gash on the back of his head. The doc says if Jake survives the next few days, he might pull through."

"I should have been there. It's not your job to do my work on the ranch with everything else you have to do."

"Gabriel already explained why you brought Cobb to town. If the situation was reversed, and Brenna was in Amanda's place, I'd do the same thing. I nearly killed a man for insulting Brenna, and that was the first day I met her. Believe me, I understand."

Ben watched Ethan's inscrutable expression shift to anger, evident only by the tightening of his jaw. He knew exactly what Ethan went through when Brenna was kidnapped because he'd been there. They'd all risked their lives—and would do so again—to bring Brenna home. Except, Ben admitted to himself, it was different with Amanda. It took all his strength not to hunt Irving and end this his way. Except, it's not what Amanda would want.

"Ethan, I want to—" Ben stepped back, out of the moonlight, and stared down the street toward the boardinghouse. "Looks like you'll get that talk with Cobb right now."

"YOU'LL DIG A FURROW in the wood with your pacing."

Amanda stopped and on reflex, looked at the boards. While Brenna's prediction had been an exaggeration, she did stop. Brenna sat in one of the chairs on the expansive porch, rocking her baby from side to side. Except for the usual evening sounds of animals and nature, the ranch was quiet.

Gabriel had gone home to be with Isabelle—ran home after Catie told him Isabelle had been having a few pains. He'd spent half the afternoon in and out of the bunkhouse, but why, no one would say. Ramsey had been to the main house twice, but otherwise no one had seen him. Eliza stopped in earlier before heading to the stables where she planned to spend the day with a few mares who were ready to foal.

Ben was suspiciously gone, as was Ethan, and when Amanda went to the barn to speak with Cobb, she'd found the space empty.

Her pacing was warranted. "Are you not curious where everyone is? Why would

Cobb not be tied up, unless they've all decided to go ahead with a plan of their doing?" Amanda sat in the other chair and stared out over the pasture. Everything was too quiet. The men worked, the cattle grazed, and nothing else needed to be done inside at the moment. Amanda sensed a rise in annoyance and quickly tempered it. "Why would they not tell us what's going on?"

Brenna seemed too calm in Amanda's opinion and sounded it when she said in her lovely Scottish accent, "As ma da use to say, 'Nae man kens how tae ease a wumman's mind, sae he daesna ettle at.'"

Amanda opened her mouth to speak, only she had no way to respond. She blew out a breath and laughed. "I have no idea what you just said."

"My father only said it when he'd vexed my mother and didn't know what else to say. It means when a man doesn't know what to say—or the right thing to say—

then he doesn't try. Whenever Ethan thinks I'm in danger, hurt, or sad, it bothers him greatly. I know it's the same for Gabe and Ramsey. They'll do everything they can to make the hurt go away, and when they can't, they do whatever they feel is right."

"Without telling you?"

Brenna nodded, a smile touching her lips. "Ethan gets around to it, and he discusses most everything with me, but there are times when he forgets until after the deed is done."

Amanda studied Brenna, curious about a hidden meaning in what she'd just said. "You know where Ethan and Ben are right now, don't you?"

"Not precisely. Ethan told me he was going to find Ben and Cobb, and he'd be home as soon as he could."

Amanda stood and smoothed down the skirts of her muted green-and-red striped dress. "I'm not helpless."

"No one believes you are."

"I had a plan, a good plan to draw out Irving."

"Yes, you did."

"You're awfully agreeable."

Brenna continued to rock her baby and smile.

"I'm being unreasonable, that's what you're thinking." Amanda continued without giving Brenna a chance to respond. "They agreed to it, Brenna. Why would they change their minds?" Amanda walked toward the edge of the porch and stood at the railing. She watched from a distance as Colton stepped out of the bunkhouse. "I'll be right back." Amanda walked down the steps and hurried toward Colton. His hand was on the saddle horn when she approached him.

"What's going on?"

Colton released the saddle and smoothed a hand over the paint's neck. They'd become friends, she and Colton, since her arrival, and she knew he and Ben were as close as any two friends on the ranch. During his initial silence, she wondered if he would tell her anything. Colton was saved from explaining when Ramsey and Eliza joined them.

Amanda looked up and held a hand at her brow to block the glare from the sun. In her haste, she'd forgotten a hat. Both sat atop their horses when they rode toward them. Ramsey dismounted a few feet away.

Colton said to Amanda, "I told them you'd figure it out." He chuckled and pulled himself into the saddle with ease. He tipped his hat and rode away.

Left alone with Ramsey and Eliza, she waited for one of them to speak. Eliza swung down from her horse, a beautiful white mare Amanda hadn't seen before. On impulse, she reached out with her hand, gave the animal a chance to accept her, and rubbed a hand smoothly over her nose. "She's beautiful."

"Part of the new breeding stock we acquired last month." Eliza watched the horse as she spoke the words. "She's a good riding horse." Eliza looked up, her inscrutable eyes focused now on Amanda. "Jake was hurt." Eliza nudged her husband. "I just found out myself and gave this one a talking to, so I've saved you from that. Though I can't say Ben will be safe when he returns."

Amanda waded through Eliza's words but remained focused on one part. She asked Ramsey, "Jake was hurt? How badly?"

Ramsey glanced at his wife with one of those looks only married couples seemed to understand. "It happened yesterday afternoon. We suspect he came upon someone in the west grazing pasture, where he was found."

"What happened to him?"

"Knife wound and a gash on the back of

his head. Doc Brody says he'll make it."

Amanda sensed more had been left unspoken. "Why the secrecy? Cobb isn't here, and he's been watched closely, so it couldn't have been him. Rustlers?"

"There's suspicion that it could still be related."

"Eliza."

Amanda caught the note of warning in her husband's tone.

"She deserves to know," Eliza said. "It's possible Irving sent someone else while waiting for Cobb."

Amanda's head shook back and forth in slow motion. She didn't believe it. Even if Irving wanted her to disappear, money only motivated a person so much. To send someone else just to see her dead would imply hatred or a deeper resentment of her.

"No, it can't be Irving. It's just gold. Cobb might have claimed he was desperate for my land, and I certainly have reason to despise the man, especially after my father's death, but none of this makes sense." She looked back and forth between the two. "It's only money."

"Money, love, and hate are the most powerful motivators for evil," Ramsey said. "Your plan to draw Irving out is a good one, but I don't think you'll have to do anything. One way or another, this is going to come to us."

"I've put you all in terrible danger."

Eliza wrapped an arm around Amanda's shouders and gave her a sisterly hug. "We've been in worse. One thing I've learned is, the best way to defeat any enemy is to go on living. Be cautious, but don't spend every day worrying about what this Irving may or may not do."

"It's not that easy, Eliza."

"No, it's not, but if the rest of us hadn't, Ethan wouldn't have Brenna, I wouldn't have Ramsey, and—"

"All right." Amanda smiled and

returned Eliza's embrace. "I get it. Trouble will come whether I worry about it or not. But Cobb is here."

"Trust Ben to know what he's doing." Ramsey lifted her chin and looked directly into her eyes. She always imagined what it would have been like to have siblings, and now she had many. "He needs to do this as much as you do, Amanda. Give him the opportunity to see this through."

24

AMANDA THOUGHT OF LITTLE more than Ramsey's words for the next hour, though it wasn't long before she found herself baking alongside Elizabeth who wanted to show her the secrets to her apple and berry cobbler.

Catie burst into the kitchen through the back door, letting in a few raindrops before she closed the portal and hung up her hat.

"Catie, what on earth are you doing walking in this weather?" Elizabeth wiped flour from her hands and passed a dry cloth to the girl. "The rain will be coming down soon."

"Gabriel said it could be a big storm!" Catie sounded pleased with the possibility of a downpour. "I wanted to see the baby. Is she awake?"

Amanda handed the girl a cup of hot chocolate and told her to sit down for a minute. "Catch your breath and warm up a bit before you go upstairs. Brenna and the baby lay down an hour ago for a nap, so you have some time. How is Isabelle?" Amanda looked at the light drizzle outside and wondered if she had time to make it to the other house. "I hoped to visit her today."

"She's resting. Gabriel said he and Andrew would look out for her for the rest of the day." Catie giggled. "She said if she gets any bigger, Gabriel is going to have build a bigger door."

Amanda didn't know enough about children—and certainly nothing about pregnancy—to sympathize with Isabelle's discomfort, but she could imagine the inconvenience of not being able to move around with ease. "She is rather large, isn't she?" Amanda whispered to Elizabeth.

"Could be a big baby she's carrying, considering the father, and Isabelle's a tall one."

"Is she going to have the baby soon?" Catie asked no one in particular.

"You'll meet the child just as soon as he or she is ready to meet you." Elizabeth set a bowl of unmixed batter in front of Catie. "You've a little time yet. I'm teaching Amanda how to make my famous cobbler. After that, you can learn how to make those oatmeal cookies you like so much."

Catie nodded with enthusiasm, slipped on an apron, and set about following Elizabeth's instructions. Amanda didn't know where the older woman found the energy every morning. Ethan joked once that Elizabeth would outlive them all, and considering her vitality, Amanda almost believed it possible.

Two hours later, when the first batch of Catie's oatmeal cookies came out of the oven, Amanda placed a few in a cloth and added the tied bundle to the basket she planned to take to Isabelle and Gabriel's house. The rain had eased, making way for the sun to peek through the white and gray clouds. The storm Gabriel had predicted seemed to have passed them by.

Amanda wrapped a shawl around her shoulders and secured her hat in place before picking up the basket. "I won't be too long. I'll visit with Isabelle for a bit if she's up to it, and I'll gather the eggs on my way back."

Elizabeth and Catie barely cast her a glance, so engrossed they were with a new recipe. It would seem cookies and cobbler weren't the only treats Catie would learn to make today.

Amanda stepped into the sunshine and looked up. A brilliant rainbow had formed over the pasture, and the cattle beneath it gave no heed to the small miracle. Fresh dew dampened the edge of her skirts as she walked over the grassy trail to Gabriel and Isabelle's house. When she reached the small, wooden bridge over the creek, she stopped, as she often did, and soaked in the landscape.

Life in the Black Hills with her father had been good and peaceful, but she wished he'd had the chance to see Montana. She didn't believe her father ever regretted the choice to remain in Dakota Territory rather than continue west. He'd loved Amanda's mother too much for disappointment to take root, no matter their reasons for settling. They'd had a wonderful life together, and though Amanda would give up the past nine months to have her father back, she somehow sensed this was where she was always meant to come.

Her reprieve from the thunderous storm was short-lived. She watched the dark clouds roll back in, swallowing the colorful rainbow, and bringing with it a biting wind. The spring meadows and tall grass quickly turned to dark shadows as the first clap of thunder resounded through the sky. The warning came only seconds before the sky unleashed hard pellets of rain.

Gabriel's house was closer, but not close enough. The force of wind and wood already slick from the rain propelled Amanda off the bridge and onto the rocky creek bed.

"Amanda!"

She loved his voice, so comforting and strong.

"Please, Amanda! Can you hear me? That's it, open your eyes."

The rain no longer pounded on her face, though she still felt the wind and the cold. Water no longer enveloped her as she lay on the wet grass. The dark form above her kept the worst of the storm away from her.

She tried to lift an arm to massage the pain from her head, but the effort was too great. "Ben?"

"It's me." Ben smoothed back the damp hair from her face, droplets of water falling from his hat. "Ethan is here, too. I need to move you to the house. Does anything hurt? Your legs, your back?"

She remembered the sudden storm, the fall into the creek. "My head and my arm."

"This arm?" At her nod, he moved up and down the length of it. When he reached behind her right shoulder, a searing pain coursed through her upper body.

"I need to move you forward, just a little, so I can take a look at your back."

She nodded again and held onto him as he brought her toward him. Amanda was now cocooned next to his body. She never wanted to leave his warmth, his protection. He slowly lowered her back down. "I'm going to lift you now. It'll hurt, but you have to stay with me, stay awake. Can you do that?"

Amanda wasn't certain of anything except she trusted Ben to do whatever necessary. She curled into him as he lifted her from the soaked ground, using her good arm to wrap around his neck. The storm continued to rage around them, and Amanda swore she felt a snowflake touch her cheek.

It wasn't until Ben handed her to someone else so he could climb onto his gelding that she saw Ethan standing by the horses. Another pain shot through her shoulder and back when Ethan lifted her into Ben's arms.

"Ben, I'm so sorry. I can't stay—" The last thing Amanda saw was a flash of lightning before she fell against Ben's chest and welcomed the darkness.

BEN WATCHED HER RETURN to him, one slow agonizing second after another until her eyes opened fully. Her beautiful amber eyes stared upward, though not directly at him, as she appeared to gauge her surroundings.

"You scared us." Scared me to the point where I thought my heart would stop, Ben thought. He held her hand, and when she shifted, she made no move to break their connection.

"What happened? It was just a fall."

Ben helped her to sit up and placed another pillow behind her back.

"Not just a fall," Eliza said from the end of the bed. Elizabeth, Brenna, and Catie had all been in and out of the room since yesterday when he had carried Amanda into the house, refusing to let Ethan or anyone help him. "The doc pulled a bullet out of your shoulder."

Ben spared a glance for Eliza who shrugged. "She would have found out and better now than later." Eliza walked around the side of the bed. To Ben, Eliza looked fighting mad, as had everyone else who learned of what happened. That is, the mad took over once they'd realized they weren't going to lose her.

"I was shot?" Amanda struggled to sit up a little higher. "Someone shot me? I didn't hear anything, and I didn't feel . . . I could have sworn it was the wind."

"You wouldn't have heard a bullet through the thunder. Whoever took the shot knew what they were doing." Any trace of the shooter had been washed away in the storm. Colton found only a few broken branches in the bushes near where the man must have hidden.

Amanda looked first at Eliza, then at Ben. "The doctor is spending more time here than in town these days. I've done this. Cobb must have—"

"No, it wasn't Cobb. He rode back from town with me and Ethan, and Colton's been with him ever since," Ben said.

"How did you find me out there? No

one would have been outside after the storm started."

"Catie and Elizabeth thought you were with Isabelle, but when you didn't come back, Catie decided to go looking for you."

"She went out in the storm?"

Ben gently pressed Amanda into the pillows when she tried to get out of bed. "No, we arrived as she was getting ready to look for you."

"Ramsey and I have talked, and we're going to move into the house until everything with Irving is settled. Isabelle is afraid to move around too much, and Gabriel needs to stay with her."

"How is Isabelle?"

Both Eliza and Ben hesitated before he said, "Isabelle thought she was going into labor last night, but it turned out to be . . . whatever false labor means. She's all right, but Gabriel isn't leaving her side right now." Ben really didn't want to talk about something he could barely form into thoughts, let alone words. There was a reason doctors kept husbands waiting outside the bedroom during childbirth. He shuddered inwardly, knowing he'd be there . . . Amanda. He was thinking of Amanda, and how it would be when she gave birth to their children.

Slow down, he told himself. Ben believed he knew where they would end up, but he still had Amanda to convince—and had to make her safe.

Eliza smirked and took pity on him. "What Ben is trying to say is that Isabelle could have the baby at any time and she decided she prefers to be around the whole family. She and Gabriel are temporarily moving back to the main house today. Catie wanted to stay with Isabelle and help, but she won't be able to if Isabelle goes into—" She glanced at Ben. "If the baby comes."

Ben found he could smile. He'd seen Eliza help birth cows and horses, so either she decided to spare him or the topic wasn't an easy one for all women. He turned his attention back to Amanda. "Are you sure you're feeling all right? You're not in pain? Doc Brody stayed the night and finally went to sleep a few hours ago."

"The pain is telling me I'm alive, and that's enough." She squeezed Ben's hand. "Somehow I always thought getting shot would hurt more."

AMANDA ENJOYED A VISIT from Brenna and the baby, two from Catie, and another from Ben who walked into the bedroom with Ethan and Ramsey. She had managed to change out of her nightgown and robe with a little help and now sat in a chair by the window. Her arm had pained her enough for the doctor to give her a white powder mixed with water and tell her to drink plenty of willow bark tea. He'd left a pouch and told her to rest, otherwise she might tear her sutures.

"Either you've all missed me or you're worried I'll be shot again." Her attempt at bringing smiles to their grim expressions didn't work. "What's happened?"

Ethan spoke first. "Forest Lloyd, the telegraph operator's son, rode out to the ranch a short while ago to deliver a telegram to Cobb."

Amanda already didn't like the direction this conversation was headed. "From Irving?"

Ramsey nodded. "Irving told Cobb not to worry about the job and to come back to Iron City."

"Which confirms Irving sent someone else." Amanda didn't need to see their hesitant nods of confirmation to know what they'd already suspected. "I'm still not convinced getting my land is enough reason for him to want me dead. Force me to sell, but kill me? I know you said money is a powerful motivation, but Irving is already rich."

Ben stepped around the other two, focused wholly on her, and moved a wooden chair from against the wall. He sat down next to her at the window and reached for her hand. "Ramsey—oddly enough with Cobb's help—may have figured that out."

Amanda braced herself for whatever he was about to say.

"Irving's desperation—his reason for coming after you—isn't exactly what we expected."

25

AMANDA DIDN'T WANT TO give Irving a single thought. She'd decided, during the many hours she was forced to stay in bed, to simply give the banker the land. It's what her parents would have wanted rather than continue to risk her life. If the land was all Irving really wanted, she'd sign everything over to him and go back to a quiet life at Hawk's Peak where she wouldn't have to look over her shoulder, wonder if someone was waiting in the shadows.

One does not miss what one does not have, her father would say. Amanda might tell herself she'd return someday to Iron

City and the land, but she couldn't imagine it now.

Of course, the reality was never as easy as one imagines. She would not disgrace her father, herself, or this family by giving in to such a person, no matter how much easier it would be.

"What do you mean?"

Ben remained by her side while Ramsey explained. "Baldwin Irving owns a share of the Iron City mine, a little under half to be exact."

Amanda nodded. "I knew this. The whole town knows. Irving built a big house and put together a celebration for the miners and their families shortly after his announcement."

"The big house, his shares, all of it, may not be his for much longer," Ethan said.

"I don't understand. He never had—"

"He had the money and a lot of it." Ramsey stepped another foot closer. "We had an investigator—one we used before by the name of Jeb Clancy—look into Irving's background. We all thought it was best to have as much information as possible, including proof of any wrongdoings, before turning him over to the authorities."

Amanda couldn't imagine the expense they'd gone through. She understood their reasons. They'd spent years waiting for the day when Nathan Hunter would make a mistake, giving them the proof they needed to send him to prison. He'd eluded them, year after year. Plenty of hirelings had been found guilty and ended up in one jail or another, but Hunter had remained untouched.

"Why didn't you tell me?"

Ethan said, "We wanted to be sure something would come of it. Irving may be evil, but lucky for us he's mostly just been a rich banker who didn't think he could be touched."

It didn't matter what they'd done

because they'd done it for her, for their family, and she had no right to be upset over it.

"What exactly did this investigator find out?"

Ben drew her attention when he spoke this time. "Not everyone is willing to talk, but it wasn't too difficult for him to find out that Irving owes a lot of money to a lot of wealthy people. He's frantic, and because your land is where the gold most likely is, he'll do anything to get it."

Amanda's earlier idea of just giving the land over held more merit, though the thought quickly passed. She would not sanction Irving's actions by giving in to him. "If we went to the marshal now, told him what you've told me, can't they look into Irving's actions?"

"They already are."

Amanda shifted to look at Ramsey. "What do you mean?"

"I spoke with my contact at the U.S.

Marshals, and the bank where Irving works has him under investigation by the Pinkerton National Detective Agency. They hired the Pinkertons to find money they believe Irving embezzled, only they can't prove it, yet. Apparently the bank is worried if Irving did in fact steal the money—and they wouldn't say how much—they'll never see it again. It seems they prefer to find the money."

Amanda's shoulder throbbed and with it came the start of an ache through her neck and head. "You mean it's possible his desperation for my land is so he'll have enough gold to put the money back into the bank and avoid going to prison?" The whole mess sounded so preposterous to have been fabricated that it held a measure of truth.

"That's what all of this looks like," Ramsey said. "Of course, only Irving can confirm the story, and he's not likely to confess to anything."

"How long has he been under investigation?" she asked Ramsey, thinking he'd most likely have the answer.

"Six months."

"And they've found nothing to prove his crimes, in all this time? If they've been watching him, how could they not realize what else he's done? My father . . ."

Ben said, "He's had a lot of help covering up his misdeeds. He won't be able to pay his men for much longer, which means he may try something on his own and slip up."

"Cobb is one of those men." Amanda saw Ben nod, but she already knew that because of Cobb and others like him on Irving's payroll, he'd been able to get away with killing her father. She had no doubt—none at all—that Baldwin Irving was responsible. She couldn't imagine ever being so desperate, and she prayed she never had to find out. "You said Sheriff Cobb helped. How?"

Ethan crossed his long arms over a wide chest. "He told us where to look."

Amanda didn't hide her skepticism. "He volunteered to help you?"

She didn't miss the brief exchange between Ben and Ethan.

"We came to an understanding." It was all Ethan would say, and Amanda decided she didn't need the details. Her body hurt, her heart ached . . . what a mess.

"What now? Do I go on, not worry about what he might do, and leave it to these Pinkertons?"

Ben shook head and leaned closer. "No, we do what you wanted to do from the beginning."

Amanda held her breath a few seconds longer than necessary. "And that is?"

"We make him come to you."

AMANDA SAT ON THE front porch, enjoying some quiet time alone. Catie sat upstairs entertaining Isabelle, who had been safely moved to the main house along with Andrew. Amanda longed for a long walk in the meadow beneath the blue sky but had promised not to go farther than the corrals, the distance the doctor seemed to think she could risk walking without causing additional injury to her wound.

When she had asked Ben exactly how bad the gunshot had been, he'd avoided answering her. She asked again, and his words shook her. He'd thought she was dead when he found her, and all she remembered was his strong arms lifting her and holding her body close to his. He'd been her buffer against the storm and against fear.

Ben approached the porch alone. He looked as though he'd been riding, and one of his hands was wrapped with a bandana.

"What happened to your hand?"

He shrugged away the notion that it was a cause for concern. "Cut it on a nail. I wasn't concentrating. How are you feeling?"

"Like I could get back to work. I need something to occupy my mind or else I'll go mad from all this recuperating."

Ben walked up the porch steps. He didn't sit down next to her as she hoped he would but leaned against the railing instead. "If all goes as planned, you'll have your answers and finally be able to move forward."

"Do you trust him?"

"I trust Ramsey. He'll make sure Cobb does what he's supposed to."

Amanda had balked when they told her the plan they'd concocted. True, it had been her idea to draw out Irving, make him come to her, but that hadn't materialized as she'd hoped. To put their belief in Cobb now . . . "I just want to know why. I relive that night in my father's store over and over, and I can't help but think it could have been avoided. If I hadn't left the back office of the store, if I'd stayed quiet, he might still be alive."

"No." Ben pushed away from the railing and sat in the chair next to her. He didn't stop there. He held her hand and gave it a little squeeze. "Don't ever blame yourself for your father's death. If it hadn't been one night, it would have been another. They would not have stopped until they had the land and the gold. Irving has proven just how far he's willing to go."

"Is that how Nathan Hunter managed to elude the law for so many years? The family doesn't speak of the details, but he did so many horrible—"

"Hunter was an evil man, yes, but Irving isn't as tough or smart as Hunter was. I know because I watched him come after the family, a little at a time. The only thing he wanted was to destroy them, and he was patient. He disappeared, and for a time, we all thought he'd leave them alone. Irving doesn't have the luxury of patience."

Her eyes met his, warm and comforting, and she knew he believed what he said. "You're saying my father would have died, no matter what?"

"I'm saying when my mother died, I blamed myself for a long time."

Amanda felt the tightening of his grip in her hand and sensed he struggled with sharing his feelings about his mother's death. He'd shared so little about his past, and she longed to know more about him.

He continued, but not without some hesitation. "I went to work for a neighbor, branding his cattle. I wanted to learn all about ranching, and my father wasn't a man who worked hard. Our neighbor was a decent man with a small operation, and I told my father I wanted to work a few days a week at the ranch. I was almost sixteen. He didn't like the idea at first, but the extra money I'd bring home swayed him in the end."

Amanda scooted closer to Ben. She said nothing but wanted him to know she was there for him.

"After a few months, I noticed my mother was quieter than usual, and my father didn't yell as often. I returned home a day early because of some bad weather and found my mother on the floor, her lip bleeding and one of her eyes swollen. She was crying. He stood over her, his fist raised to strike again. When he saw me in the doorway, he looked shocked, and then he turned angry. Angrier than I'd ever seen him. I wasn't as big as him, but I was strong and gave him the same punishment he thought my mother deserved. I quit work at the ranch and made sure my father never hurt my mother again."

She wanted to say something, anything to comfort him, but no words came. Amanda didn't think any words could make the retelling of such awful memories any easier. He pulled his focus away from the landscape beyond the porch and faced her.

"She died a few weeks later, and the doctor said it was from injuries we couldn't see. No matter how often I relive those weeks or ask myself what I could have done differently, it won't bring her back. It won't change what happened, and what's more, she wouldn't have wanted me to blame myself. And neither would your father."

"What happened to your father?"

The seconds lasted too long as she waited.

"He left the day after I threatened to kill him if he ever laid another hand on my mother. I never saw him again."

Her heart ached for Ben and what he'd gone through as a young man. She'd been lucky. He was right. Her father wouldn't want her to ever question or lay blame on herself. She lifted her good arm and spread her pale hand over his tanned cheek. He leaned into her touch and kissed her palm.

"Everything will work out, Amanda."

Tears that had accumulated during his story now fell one by one. "I know."

26

THREE DAYS PASSED WITHOUT incident. The sun chose to shine and the days warmed, scaring away any chance of another spring snowfall. Of course, Amanda knew how quickly the unexpected could sneak up on a person. Her shoulder was healing, though not as quickly as she would have liked. When the doctor left the morning after she awakened, she heard him tell Ben, "Good luck," before he chuckled and left the room.

Determined not to spend every moment of every day fretting over Ramsey and Cobb's progress, and knowing that it would still be at least a few more days before they received news, Amanda enjoyed the sunshine and spending time with Brenna.

Eliza had temporarily moved back into the main house while Ramsey was away, at both her husband and brothers' insistence, while the possible danger lurked. She left early to go work with the horses and didn't return until supper. Amanda admired her determination and her seemingly never-ending energy.

Brenna and the baby thrived, and Amanda found the extra time spent with the mother and new daughter to be both healing and enjoyable. New life and beautiful blessings always found a way to brighten the darkness.

"You appear faraway in your thoughts."

Amanda opened her eyes and looked at Brenna. Her hair spilled over her shoulders. A wide-brimmed hat perched atop her head, shielding both her face and the baby from the afternoon sun. Brenna glowed with happiness, a woman content in her love and in the future. Amanda found her thoughts shifting to Ben. "There's a lot to think about."

"I'm sure you're worried about what's happening right now in Iron City. I would be, too."

Amanda nodded and walked back toward Brenna, her fingertips skimming the top of a blackberry bush. The cooler weather had kept the blossoms at bay, but soon the white flowers would emerge. Brenna had told her that Ethan's father had planted the bushes in the family garden because his wife loved anything baked with blackberries. Amanda wondered if she'd be able to get cuttings for her own garden one day.

Her own garden? A garden would mean a home, and she had one of those right here with Brenna and Ethan. From where had that thought come? Amanda wondered before she shook it away. "They traveled by train from Bozeman, and once off the train, the ride to Iron City is only a day. What do you suppose is taking them so long?" Amanda promised herself she wouldn't worry and here she was—fretting.

"Ramsey will send word as soon as they arrive."

"It's Cobb I don't trust. What if he's—"

"They all trusted Sheriff Cobb enough to help," Brenna said, "Besides, I know my brother, and he would never let Cobb . . . what's the odd phrase he used? Oh yes, get the drop on him."

Amanda smiled and soon light laughter bubbled up. Brenna had first left Scotland more than two years ago, and though some of the time had been spent back in her homeland, it never failed to amuse Amanda when Brenna attempted to mimic the slower accents found in the West. "No, Ramsey wouldn't allow it." She stood next to Brenna now and peeked beneath the blanket to gaze upon Rebecca's sleeping face.

"She's peaceful, as though she knows there's nothing in this world that could ever harm her. I envy her." When Amanda looked back, she found Brenna staring at her.

"Her father, not to mention her uncles and everyone else here, would never let someone do her harm. The same holds true for everyone in this family."

"Speaking of family, I should see to lunch."

"You'll do no such thing," Brenna told her. "I realize we're all better off when I don't spend too much in the kitchen, but I can manage lunch while you enjoy a little time with Rebecca. Ethan will stop in soon enough—the man can't go two hours without checking on us—and I imagine Ben will be with him."

Amanda smiled, hoping it was true.

She'd spent more and more time thinking about Ben Stuart. She had thought to wait before she told him how she felt, believing if she had to run again, her departure after a confession of her feelings wouldn't be fair to him . . . or her.

AMANDA FOLLOWED BEN OUTSIDE. He'd accepted the offer of lunch, but in her mind, their time together ended too quickly. She enjoyed the calm and comfort she felt when he was around and would have enjoyed more time. He stopped and turned at the base of the porch steps.

"You mentioned to Brenna that you would like to go into town this afternoon."

Amanda tucked her hands in the edges of her shawl. "I've missed a few days helping at the school because of my injury and everything with Irving, and I'd like to go back. Catie could use a visit with some of her friends as well."

"It's safer for you to stay here at the

ranch, at least until Ramsey and Cobb return and we have a clearer picture of what is going on."

"We don't know how long that will be. Didn't you tell me to keep my days as normal as possible?"

Ben removed his hat and snaked a hand through his unruly, dark hair. "That was before you were shot."

"Normal is what I need to feel right now. Please, Ben. I hope you understand."

"Then I'm going into town with you. You can stay at the cottage and I'll bunk in the wagon outside."

She knew it would be useless to argue with him. "Thank you."

CATIE'S EXCITEMENT AT THE prospect of returning to town became contagious, though Amanda suspected her eagerness had more to do with seeing Cord and less to do with the upcoming play. Ben even smiled as Catie chattered on about the play, Cord, his mother, and how she hoped she'd get to see Phineas Simms' new puppies.

They rolled into town a few hours before dark would set in, and Ben pulled to a stop in front of the cottage. "I want to check in at the telegraph office while we're here."

Amanda didn't need to hear him say that he hoped for news from Ramsey as much as she did. "We'll get settled inside, and then I'll walk Catie to the school."

Ben hesitated, and she thought he might not leave them alone. "You won't go anywhere else except the school?" He helped Catie down from the wagon first, and with his arms around Amanda's waist, he lifted her to the ground.

"I promise."

His hands lingered for a few seconds before he stepped back. "I won't be long." He carried the single valise and a basket of food Amanda had prepared for the evening into the cottage. Catie followed him inside while Amanda waited with the horses, enjoying a few minutes alone.

Ben brushed a hand over her arm before he climbed back into the wagon. She watched him turn the wagon and drive around the corner to the telegraph office. From her vantage point in front of the cottage, she could see a large portion of the small town of Briarwood, but if she walked a few feet in either direction, the cottage's location amongst the towering pines offered a peaceful retreat. The rocky creek of clear mountain water that gurgled and flowed nearby was the only sound to intrude upon the quiet.

Amanda joined Catie inside and found the girl had placed a few items in the icebox and set Amanda's bag on the bed in the larger of the two bedrooms.

"Can we go to the school now? Maybe Cord is there waiting."

"May we," Amanda corrected, "and

yes." They stepped outside where a light breeze had formed. "Perhaps we'll have another storm." Amanda hoped not. She enjoyed storms, the torrential temper of nature, but she thought of what Ben had said about sleeping in the wagon outside the cottage.

Amanda locked the side door to the cottage and joined Catie on the edge of the meadow that separated the cottage from the school and town. "If Cord isn't at the schoolhouse, we'll visit him at—what's wrong, Catie?" The girl appeared terrified, and Amanda turned to see what had caught her attention.

Amanda's throat constricted and her heartbeat escalated.

"You didn't think I'd forget about my sweet honey-haired beauty, did you?"

Amanda stepped in front of Catie, blocking his view of the younger girl. "How?"

"It doesn't matter how. We'll have

plenty of time for talking where we're going."

Amanda considered all of her options, but even the best of them didn't seem promising. "I'll scream and someone will hear me."

"Are you talking about the cowboy who drove away? I don't think he'll bother us, seeing as how he's on the other side of town. I made sure we were alone. Now, you're going to come quietly." He trained a pistol on Catie. "If you want this pretty one to live."

Amanda didn't know how he'd made it so close to the cottage without being seen. He timed his arrival well. Too well for it not to have been planned. How long had he been watching, waiting for her to leave the ranch? Then again, she had to remember who she was dealing with. "Catie, go inside and close the door." Amanda slipped the girl the key.

"Catie. Such a pretty name. Don't go

inside, Catie. Lie down on the ground."

"Don't you dare do this. Kill me if that's your plan, but you won't hurt her." Amanda stepped backward until she was directly in front of Catie. The edges of her long coat flapped in the wind. "Go inside, Catie."

Amanda heard the familiar click of the hammer on the pistol and froze.

"You think I'll stop with you? I could shoot you and take the girl. They may come after me, but not before I kill her . . . after a time."

Amanda felt tears burn the back of her eyes. "Catie, lie down on the ground. It's okay, sweetheart." She heard the girl's quiet shudders of breath but didn't dare turn around. If she could stall him just a little longer, someone might drive on the nearby road into town. Just a little—

"Step over here and put your foot in the stirrup."

He motioned her over but kept the gun

trained on Catie, not her. When Amanda realized his plan was to have her sit on his lap, she tried to move away. He yanked her up and quickly tied a cloth around her mouth. "Now, little Catie girl. If you don't want me to put a bullet in Amanda, you'll be real quiet. Do you hear?"

Catie lay flat to the ground, her face in the grass. When she heard the horse nicker, she turned her head to see them ride away. She pushed off the ground and ran toward town—and Ben—as fast as she could.

27

BEN TUCKED THE TELEGRAM into the pocket of his brown duster. "Thank you, Orin."

"You're welcome, Ben. By the way, had a fellow in here asking about ranch work in these parts. He asked if Hawk's Peak was hiring."

It wasn't unusual for the occasional out-of-work cowboy to find his way into Briarwood, looking for a job. "No one has come out to the ranch asking about work. When did they pass through?"

"A couple of days before the storm. He didn't look down on his luck, so maybe he didn't need the work after all."

Ben turned his attention to the two windows at the front of the telegraph office. Both offered an unobstructed view of the boardwalk and a good portion of the street in front. Despite the growing territory, their small town had managed to remain somewhat isolated. Hawk's Peak was well enough known in Montana for its size and the reputation of the Gallagher family, but it was also known for not arbitrarily taking on any drifter who sought work.

He turned back to Orin. "Have you seen him again since?"

"Sure, a couple of times outside the saloon and once in the general store. Doesn't seem in a hurry to leave if you want to talk to him. He's not too tall but looks strong. Might be a good worker."

Ben wasn't interested in hiring anyone new and neither was Ethan. Levi Gibbs should work out fine, and Ben preferred to give the young man a chance before they looked for someone else. However, he did want to meet this cowboy. "Appreciate your time, Orin." He exited the building and stepped onto the boardwalk. No one lingered in front of any buildings, but it was still early. Another hour or two and a few more men would make their way over to the saloon where Millie would serve drinks and the men would gamble away what little they made from odd jobs.

He entered the saloon and went directly to the bar where Millie wiped down glasses. "Any word from your brother?"

She scoffed and offered him a drink, which Ben declined. "That good-for-nothing wrote a letter, said he's in San Francisco. Wants nothing more to do with this place."

Ben looked around the interior, and although dark and in need of a few repairs, Millie had kept it up in her brother's absence. She didn't tolerate fighting or swearing, and the town had a law against prostitution, so she didn't have to worry about that element making its way into her establishment. "You could do worse."

"I know it. Hired me a man a few days ago to keep order during our busier hours."

Curious, Ben thought. "Did you do any checking up on him?"

"He's not bad looking, good with a gun, and stronger than he looks. If he gets the job done and doesn't steal from me, then what do I care about his past?"

Ben could appreciate Millie giving someone a second chance, if that's why the man was in Briarwood, but it wouldn't hurt to make a few inquiries on her behalf. "Where is this new employee? I'd like to meet him."

"Don't you go causing me trouble, Ben Stuart. You and them other boys at the ranch don't give me any business, but these other boys here do. I'd just as soon as keep them coming."

Ben held up his hands. "I'm just trying to help. In fact, I wanted to ask if a stranger has been into the saloon in the past week. Would have stopped in a day or two before the storm hit, maybe after." Ben used Orin's description of the man. "Not too tall but looks strong."

Millie set down her cloth and the glass she was cleaning. "Could be Tucker, the new man I hired. What do you want with him?"

"Orin said the man was looking for ranch work. Looks like he found a job here instead."

Millie shrugged and refilled one of her patron's glasses before turning back to Ben. "I expect him here in an hour. You can wait."

Ben thought of Amanda and Catie and shook his head. "I'd better get—"

He heard the shouts, and so did everyone else in the saloon. Ben was the first one through the swinging saloon doors but not the only one waiting outside when Catie came running down the center of the dirt street. He ran into the road and swung her into a stop and knelt on one knee in front of her. "What's happened?"

Catie's breaths came in quick, shallow bursts. "The man. Amanda. He took her."

"Who, Catie? Where did he take her?"

"A man with a gun. I think he was waiting for Amanda." She clasped her hands onto Ben's shoulders. "I think she knew him. She made him leave me alone."

Ben's heart pounded and his skin tingled from the sudden rush of fear. "Did you see which way he took her?"

Catie nodded, a contradictory combination of terror and anger in her eyes. "He put her on his horse. They went into the trees across the meadow."

Any number of people would have seen them if they'd crossed the open field. There were only two directions they could have taken and gone unnoticed.

"Ben, what's going on?"

Ben glanced up at Otis Lincoln. A few others had gathered around, a mix of curiosity and concern etched on their faces. "I need you to ride out to the ranch, tell whoever you see I've ridden east from the Gallaghers' cottage. Colton has the best chance of picking up my trail." Ben stood and told Catie, "Stay with Mrs. Baker at the store until I come back or someone from the ranch comes to get you."

"She can stay with us, Mr. Stuart. Don't you worry."

Ben turned to see Cord Beckert standing only a few feet behind them. "All right, Cord. I'm going to trust you to look after her."

Cord walked to Catie and slipped her hand into his. "I promise, Mr. Stuart."

Catie leaned toward Ben and whispered, "You'll find her, right?"

"I'll find her."

BEN LEFT THE WAGON and borrowed a horse from Otis's livery. He rode to the cottage and picked up the trail after five minutes. He could track but lacked Colton's eye for details. If it hadn't been for the recent storm and the lack of footprints around the cottage, he might have missed the single set of hoofprints on the opposite side of the creek. Some broken branches and a few depressions in the damp earth led him along the edge of the meadow and into the woods.

On the other side of the deep forest ran a river too wide and dangerous to cross this time of year and the Black Cotter Peaks, a small range of uninhabited hills. Whoever took Amanda had a few miles of woods to ride through, and whatever horse he rode wouldn't be able to carry two people for long without resting up.

AMANDA'S THROAT ACHED FOR water.

She'd woken in the middle of night, afraid the people who killed her father would come for her. Her nightmare had come true and had been far less frightening than what she experienced now.

For every second she spent with the man, she imagined one nightmare after another. Death would be worse to some. To her, it would be preferable than what she was almost certain Reed had planned for her. She would have gone with him again, if it meant saving Catie. Amanda didn't believe he would have killed the young girl, but the rape and the ruination of everything good in the child . . . those were things she couldn't allow.

Would it be her fate now? Would someone realize what had happened in time to catch up with them? She tried to study the landscape, figure out where they were going, but she'd never been on this side of town or in these woods. If she could get away, Amanda wasn't certain she could find her way back. Anywhere else was better than here.

Reed Slater's arms circled her waist, holding her firmly against his chest, despite her efforts to push away. The air grew colder the farther into the forest they rode. The poor horse didn't look strong enough to travel far, let alone be put through the strain of carrying their combined weight. She saw where Reed's spurs had cut up the animal's flank.

She twisted in his grip. Falling onto the ground would be preferable to remaining in his arms.

"Stop that!" His words came out as a harsh hiss.

Amanda continued to move, and the horse halted, shifting on its legs. Reed climbed down and pulled Amanda with him. When he yanked down the cloth around her mouth, she heaved in fresh air and attempted to moisten her dry throat. "Keep your hands off me!"

She didn't expect the force of his open palm to topple her. Amanda glared up at him from where she'd fallen on twigs, rocks, and damp grass. Patches of snow lingered beneath the thick canopy of trees where the sun's rays couldn't reach.

Amanda didn't need to ask why he'd followed her, taken her, but how did he find her? "They'll find you."

He twisted her hair in his hands and pulled with such force, tears formed in her eyes. "You think I care about the ranchers? Yeah, I know about them." He shoved her away. "All high and mighty they think they are, just like those Bible-lovin' churchgoers on the wagon train. They thought they could send me away." Reed knelt on the ground next to her. "You almost got away in Bozeman. You shouldn't have done that, Amanda."

She watched him, certain if she spoke, her words would upset him. How could she have known when she spurned his advances, his pursuit of her would escalate?

He stood, bent over, cupping her face to the point where she felt her teeth dig into the side of her cheeks. "You weren't easy to find. I don't know why you tried to hide from me. You should have known I'd find you." He pulled her up and pressed her against him. "Did you sleep with him?" He spoke barely above a whisper, his previous anger no longer evident. "Did you lie down with that cowboy?"

Amanda took too long to answer.

"Tell me!" Reed shook her by the collar of her coat, tearing one of the seams. "Did you lie with him."

"No!"

He smoothed down her collar and with great gentleness lifted her hands to his lips. "That's my girl. I saw you kiss him. You'll have to make it up to me, but we can fix this. We can fix us."

The enormity of what was happening

forced Amanda to remain composed when she felt anything but calm. "You're not angry with me?"

He pressed his cold lips to her hands once more and smiled. "I can forgive you, but you have to promise not to leave me again."

She wondered if he could see how her body shook. She'd say anything to give herself more time, but no matter how strong anyone professed her to be, Amanda wouldn't give herself to him. She'd fight, hope, and pray someone—Ben and the others—would come for her, find her, but she couldn't give in. Her conscience wouldn't allow it. Now she had to make him believe in her weakness, her compliance. He couldn't know just how much he frightened her because then he'd have all the power.

"I promise."

Reed studied her carefully, grabbed her chin and moved his face so close to hers she thought he was going to kiss her. Instead, he stared into her eyes. His were cold, dark, and filled with rage. He stepped back a few inches, his face contorted. "I don't believe you, Amanda."

"Reed, I—"

"No! Don't lie to me." He replaced the cloth over her mouth, this time tightening it until it dug into her lips. He jerked back toward the horse and lifted her onto the saddle before climbing up behind her. "It doesn't matter. You'll learn not to lie to me soon enough. We'll be together, and you'll learn to forget your rancher man."

He turned the horse to the right and ascended the gradual incline.

BEN LOST THE TRAIL, backtracked, and managed to pick it up again. They had stopped. He pushed down his rising concern when he noticed the grass and leaves pressed down. Someone had fallen or lain here, and his only peace came from knowing they wouldn't have been able to stop long enough for the nightmare Ben imagined.

He heard a subtle shift in the wind, a crunch nearby. An animal or human? He dropped the reins, turned, and pointed his gun toward the noise.

"It's just me, Ben."

Colton moved forward on his speckled gelding.

Ben lowered his gun and replaced it in the holster. "I'm glad to see you. I don't know who this man is or why he's taken Amanda, but I need to find him now. He's already misdirected me once. I can't waste any more time."

Colton didn't respond. He dismounted and examined the ground in half the time it had taken Ben. "You're closing in on them faster than you think. They have maybe half a mile on you, and it's closing." He swung up on the back of his horse, not bothering with the stirrup. "Ethan and two of the men are riding around the forest from the north. I took a guess that whoever we're after would head for the hills rather than the river."

"Then let's make sure they don't have a way out."

28

THE SKIES OPENED AND released a lashing upon the earth, one to make the previous storm seem like a tame breeze carrying a light dew. The weary horse faltered on the muddy slope, forcing Reed to dismount and pull Amanda to her feet.

Reed loosened the tie around her mouth, though she doubted it was for her comfort. "We'll die out here!" Her voice fought against the force of the wind and sounded hoarse to her own ears. "We have to go back!"

"Shut up! We're not going back." Reed dragged her and the horse as they continued to climb the hill.

Amanda struggled to remain on her feet and couldn't see more than a few feet in front of her. The forest thinned, allowing a deluge of heavy rain to fall on them, and without protection from the cold, Amanda didn't know how long they could last. The higher they climbed, they colder it became. The day began its slow descent into evening, and when they lost those last few rays of sunshine and warmth, the cold mountain air would be merciless.

She knew Catie had gone for Ben and he would come looking for her. She prayed that by the time he found them, it wouldn't be too late.

"Reed, we have to find shelter." He pressed her up against a large pine whose branches couldn't protect them from the increasing flood of rain. "Please, Reed." She turned and faced him, desperate to reach whatever insane obsession drove him to kidnap her. "Please."

Reed didn't answer. He appeared to be

as frantic as she felt. "We keep going."

Amanda pulled with every bit of strength she possessed. Her weight and the unstable mud beneath their feet propelled her backward and Reed forward. Amanda heard the horse release what sounded like a low screech before it reared back and disappeared down the hill. She wished she could follow it.

His hand connected with her face before he rolled and struggled to pull her up with him. When they'd found their footing again, she shook from the force of the struggle.

"Don't you ever do that again!" He gripped her arm in a painful vice and continued to climb back up the hill.

A HORSE EMERGED FROM the trees, frightened and fatigued. It shied away when it saw Ben and Colton, then gestured with its head as though to acknowledge his gratitude for their presence.

Beads of water dripped off the brim of Ben's hat as he dismounted to examine the pathetic animal. The reins hanged free, and it was a miracle the horse hadn't caught his leg and floundered. Colton remained on his horse and leaned forward. "Can it walk?"

Ben nodded and tied off the reins over the gelding's neck. "He's weak but should make it back."

"This could mean—"

"I know." Ben didn't want to think of what might have happened to Amanda. Had something happened to her captor and now she was out there alone? Ben couldn't decide which was worse. He held out hope that if someone went to this much trouble to take her, they had a reason to keep her alive. "There's no way to keep to their trail with this coming down." Ben settled back in the saddle, his horse rubbing against Colton's. They were close enough to speak without shouting, but barely.

"Don't be too sure." Colton didn't offer any other reassurance. He set his sure-footed gelding back in motion and continued up the hill in the direction the other horse had come.

Ben kept telling himself that each careful step brought them closer to Amanda. Ethan and the others would either climb up from the other side of the woods or if they hadn't made it through due to the weather, stop at the base of the hill. Either way, whoever they were chasing wouldn't make it out alive.

Colton stopped without notice. He held up his hand and made a fist, indicating for Ben to stop and remain silent. They moved to the right, into a copse of trees. Ben peered through the rain. The wind persisted, but the rain had settled into a heavy drizzle. He saw them, on the outskirts of the tree line, Amanda on her knees.

SHE COULDN'T TAKE ANOTHER step. The hem of her dress, torn and filthy, tripped her, and she fell forward. Her knees and hands broke her fall, but she was beyond noticing any pain. Exhaustion had won.

"Get up." Reed pulled on her arms. She pulled back. "Get up, now!"

"Whatever you plan to do, get it over with. I'm not going any farther."

He crouched down and shook her, the tremble radiating through every part of her body. How long had it been since she left Catie alone by the cottage? A few hours? Amanda looked up to the sky. Even the setting sun couldn't offer enough light to give her hope she'd find a way to escape. The storm would have slowed anyone searching for her.

It wasn't in her to give up, but neither would she give in. The rain eased, and a thin shaft of evening light peeked through the dark clouds. The wind whipped her clothes and stirred the rest of her hair from its braid.

"Where do you plan to go? There's nowhere except over the hills, and we can't do that without a horse. We can go back, you'll leave, and no one will find you."

"You're coming with me, do you hear!" He rose and paced, oblivious to the rain and wind. "You should have been nicer to me behind the wagon that night, Amanda. Telling them what I'd done, what you accused me of, cost me my job. All you had to do was keep your mouth shut. You didn't know how good it would be with us. You thought you were smart, runnin' like you did, but I found you." He spun and shouted down at her. "I found you!"

Amanda sensed another shift, but this time not from the weather. Reed stilled, his attention on the trees. He looked in every direction before he reached down and lifted her until she stood against him. She felt his gun pressed against her side and watched the area of the woods that had drawn Reed's interest. She saw nothing.

"That's far enough."

Amanda wanted to weep and run into Ben's arms when she recognized his voice, carried to her by the wind. She saw him step from the woods, into the open meadow where she and Reed stood and waited. A few seconds later, Colton joined him.

Reed pressed his face against her hair and whispered, "He won't make it. Now you can watch him die and you'll know how much you mean to me."

She ignored Reed, her eyes focused on Ben. He didn't look her way, and she understood. His attention was on her captor.

Ben walked toward them, each step slow and steady. Colton moved to the left, splitting Reed's concentration. "Stay where you are," he called out to them. "I'll kill her."

"You're not going to kill her." Ben continued to advance, his rifle aimed, his finger on the trigger. "You're going to let her go, Slater."

How Ben figured it out, Amanda couldn't guess, and she didn't care. She kept her voice low when she spoke to Reed. "If you shoot me, your death is certain. Let me go to them."

Reed shook his head, saying "No" over and over again. Amanda felt the tip of his pistol press deeper into her side.

BEN STOOD A DOZEN feet away, close enough to risk a glance at Amanda. He needed to see in her eyes that she was all right. He didn't imagine the calm she presented or the subtle message she sent him. He wanted to tell her not to take the chance, to stay where she was until one of them got a clear shot at Slater without hurting her.

He hadn't known for sure it was Reed Slater, the man who had tried to assault her on the wagon drive from Dakota. If the man had been sent by Irving, he would have killed Amanda and left her body in the forest or dropped her in the river.

Colton stood on the other side of them, his gun pointed at Slater. When Ben spared him a glance, Colton gave him a quick shake of his head. He didn't have a clean shot.

Amanda drew his attention once more, smiled, and fell to the ground.

Ben didn't know whose bullet sent Slater to his immediate death. He dropped his rifle and rushed to Amanda. She slipped her arms around his neck and allowed him to carry her a safe distance away. He brushed back her wet hair and pressed his lips to hers. "You're all right? Did he hurt you?"

"No, nothing that won't heal." She hesitated, staring into his concerned eyes, so filled with love. "He didn't hurt me, Ben."

Ben removed his duster and enveloped her body in it. The coat was wet but would offer her some protection. Colton walked up behind them.

"You did good, Amanda."

29

AMANDA RODE IN FRONT of Ben, secure in his arms. The others rode with them in the deepening darkness, their sure-footed horses making the descent down the hill in slow and steady steps. Amanda didn't know how they saw in the dark nor did she care. She felt as though she'd been held captive with Reed for days rather than a few hours, and she wanted only to enjoy the comfort of being among family. Even more, she wanted this quest to end.

They were as close to family as her own flesh and blood had ever been. She would never again question the bond she shared with the Gallaghers and the menagerie of souls who had found a home at Hawk's Peak.

She was settled comfortably across Ben's lap and had no desire to move. When she suggested she could ride Reed's horse, Colton informed her the animal had injured its leg at some point and shouldn't be ridden. Amanda didn't mind, though she silently cursed Reed Slater for his treatment of the poor animal. Where the spotted gelding was going, he would be free to graze and live a quiet life among friends.

"Are we going to ride all the way back in the dark?"

Ben's arms shifted slightly when the horse edged around a tree.

"And how do they see in the dark? I can barely see what's a few feet in front of us."

Ben chuckled. "They have a wider field of vision than we do and catch movement better, but we're doing some of the looking for them." He didn't have to lean in to speak softly near her ear. "Under normal circumstances, we would have found shelter, waited until first light."

"Except for . . . the body." Amanda had been so grateful to be rescued, to be free of Reed, the reality that someone took a man's life in the process had yet to fully sink in. "I'm sorry you and Colton had to kill him." She didn't know which bullet ended Reed's life, and she didn't want to know.

"We're not," Ben whispered. "You should rest if you can. Now that the rain has stopped and the moon is out, we'll be back to town in a couple of hours."

Amanda wanted to ask more questions about Catie, about how they found her, but she soon found herself relaxing against Ben. Her eyes drifted closed, dimming what little light remained from the moon.

WHEN THEY RODE ONTO the ranch, Ben and Colton stopped their horses in front of the main stone-and-timber house an hour before the sun would rise. Once they'd reached town, Amanda had been sound asleep, her soft breaths heating through Ben's shirt, and he had no desire to wake her.

Catie would be asleep at the Beckerts' house, and the clouds had parted to reveal a deep blue sky resplendent with millions of bright stars and a pale, vibrant moon. Ethan told Ben to ride back to the ranch, and he'd bring Catie home because he suspected Amanda would ask once she awakened.

Once they reached Hawk's Peak, Colton dismounted first and Ben lifted Amanda into his friend's arms while he alighted from his horse. Amanda stirred in Colton's arms. "Where are we? Colton?"

Colton grinned and set her on her feet. "You'll find your bearings soon enough." He turned and guiding his horse and the one that belonged to Reed, he headed for the stable.

Ben watched her take in her surroundings and noticed the quiet sigh when she realized where she stood. Her gaze drifted to the main house and a soft smile touched her lips.

"I don't know how I could find anything to be happy about right now, but I suppose there's always something to be grateful for, isn't there?"

"I've always liked to believe so." Ben focused on her, not the house, but he understood what she meant. Since he had left home, he'd wandered for a long time. Even during the years Marge and Josiah had welcomed him into their home and kept him on a straight path when it would have been easy to stray, he'd never truly felt at home until he arrived at Hawk's Peak. "How's your shoulder?"

"There's a little pain, but rather a little then . . . well, it could have been worse."

Ben knew exactly how much worse it

could have been. During every frantic second he'd searched for her, his one comfort was the weather. As much as it hindered their rescue, it also kept Reed from doing unspeakable things to her. The delays had made Reed anxious to put as much distance between him and anyone who might be chasing them.

"You're home now, and that's what matters."

She looked up at the house once again. "I should go inside. I desperately want a bath and I imagine you're exhausted, but would you sit with me out here for a few minutes to watch the sun rise over the mountains? I wasn't sure I'd be around for another one, and I'd really like to enjoy it with you."

Ben removed his riding gloves and brushed a single tear from her cheek. He tied off his horse to the rail and enclosed her hand with his. They settled on a wooden bench set against the house on the porch. Without hesitation, Amanda leaned against Ben and laid her head on his shoulder.

"AMANDA!"

Catie seemed to fly into the room and scrambled onto the edge of the bed. Amanda wasn't certain when she had made her way inside or how long she'd slept. A bright sun, free of color, crept in through the window.

"Are you all right? Ben said you are, and Brenna promised you were only tired, but you're sure you're okay?"

Amanda patted the space next to her on the bed. "I'm all right. In truth, I feel better than I have in a long time."

Catie tilted her head one way and then the other. "You're sure? I was so scared, but I knew Ben would find you."

"And I owe my thanks to you!"

"To me?" Catie's wide-eyed curiosity brought a smile to Amanda's lips.

"Of course. You went for help and found Ben. Because of you, he found me."

Catie wrapped her arms around Amanda, knocking a startled breath from her. "Promise not to ever leave us."

Amanda eased the young girl back and brushed away an errant lock of hair. She would be a young woman soon. Already, Amanda could see the last vestiges of childhood vanishing from the girl. They may be almost a decade apart in age, but they'd both struggled on the same journey to find someplace where they could belong. The difference was that Catie had much further to travel, but she had shown strength to be envied by many women much older.

"You will go far in life, Catie. Always remember you can do anything, be anyone. You are one of the strongest people I've ever known." She leaned forward and kissed the girl's cheek. "Thank you."

Catie smiled, a beautiful and bright grin that revealed the bit of her lingering innocence. "I want to be just like you," she confessed before she skipped out of the bedroom.

I WANT TO BE just like you. Amanda believed Catie would grow up to be better and stronger. Amanda knew what lay beyond this beautiful valley—both the good and the unpleasant—and she looked forward to watching Catie and Andrew, young Jacob and Rebecca, and soon Isabelle's new baby, grow up on this land.

She walked along the edge of the creek where it met the meadow and knelt beside where she'd fallen in during the storm. Her shoulder still twinged when she moved it or lifted anything, but she considered herself lucky. Ben had cautioned her that it was unlikely Reed who would have shot her, which meant whoever had could still be waiting for another chance. His desire to have her would have been too strong to harm her. Even in the end, when he could have pulled the trigger and put a bullet in her, he'd hesitated.

Amanda realized she didn't regret Reed's death. She also knew the danger wasn't yet over and wouldn't be until she faced Irving. She stood and gazed across the glistening stream and meadow. Birds twittered and chattered in nearby trees, and somewhere beyond she heard horses. Had it not been for the houses, or the two men riding toward her, she would have believed herself completely alone.

The two Gallagher brothers were recognizable from almost any distance. She offered both a smile when they approached from the other side of the water. Neither of them returned a smile equal to her own, and she knew something was wrong.

"Has there been news?"

Ethan nodded and leaned forward on his saddle horn. "We were on our way to the house to tell both you and Ben. A telegram arrived. Irving wasn't there when Ramsey and Cobb reached Iron City. They contacted the U.S. Marshal for the Dakota Territory, but they'd lost track of Irving. Cobb's telegram said Ramsey was already on his way back here, on the train and riding alone. He should arrive soon."

Amanda looked from one brother to the next. "What do you mean by 'Cobb's telegram'? Did Ramsey leave Cobb there?"

Gabriel said, "Ramsey would have had his reasons, and he wouldn't have done it if he didn't think Cobb could be trusted. Don't worry, we've reached out to the marshal directly and should hear back in a day or two."

Amanda did trust Ramsey, but she wished she understood why he left Stratton Cobb alone when he should be held accountable for his part in so much misery. She didn't think only of her father at this moment. No matter how much she disliked Cobb, she believed he wasn't involved in her father's death. Except she couldn't discount all the other times he'd cleaned up after Irving, by his own admission.

"Is Cobb free then?"

Ethan sat up straight and shook his head. "The telegram also said he wouldn't be too far behind, that he had . . . business to clean up." Ethan dismounted and walked over the bridge with his stallion, a beautiful black Amanda marveled at every time she saw him. "Cobb will have to answer for what he's done somehow, but we have no proof he's done anything wrong."

"Except his admission."

"His admission that he did things he wasn't proud of." Ethan looked briefly back at his brother who nodded once. "We've all done things we wish we could change. Cobb came here to warn you, and none of us may like him, but we're grateful for what he did. If he can make amends for past transgressions, then he deserves the chance."

Gabriel crossed the bridge and smiled down at her. "Don't worry about Cobb right now. Irving is the greater danger. We promised to let Ben know when news came in."

Amanda released a heavy breath that had constricted around her heart. "He hasn't had much sleep."

"I told him to take it easy for a couple of days," Ethan said.

"We both know that's not Ben." She smiled at the memory of the morning before when he'd sat with her to watch the sunrise. "I saw him ride out an hour ago toward Ramsey and Eliza's cabin."

"I'll go and find him." Gabriel turned his horse when Amanda said, "I saw Isabelle this morning. She looks well.

Elizabeth thinks the baby will come early."

Gabriel's smile slackened and worry etched the area around his eyes. He had too much concern to add her worries to the mix. "She can't wait to hold the baby in her arms. Truth is, neither can I."

"Ethan?" Amanda said his name barely above a whisper. If he hadn't been standing so close, the wind would have carried it away. She wanted to think only of the family, the children, the simple and quiet life at Hawk's Peak, but she needed to know. "And if Cobb killed people, innocent people?"

Ethan swung back up on his horse. "Then I'll escort him to the hangman's noose myself."

30

BEN AWAKENED, A HAND instinctively pressed against the side of his head where the immediate pain originated. Only another pain, sharper and deeper, drew his attention. He reached down to his side and found the source. His vision blurred before it came into focus. He pulled his hand away and found the tips of his fingers covered in blood.

The cold air brushed against him, and when he tried to move, he found himself laying on a blanket of pine needles, rocks, and twigs. He looked up, a canopy of pine boughs blocking the sky. He couldn't tell the time of day.

"Thought Stutz here might have done you in when he hit your head."

Ben shifted and looked up into the face of a man he'd not met before. From the cut of the expensive clothes to the arrogant bearing, he figured he already knew who stood before him. "You can't do anything yourself, can you? Takes all of you to ambush one person."

Irving sniffed and motioned for one of his men to lift Ben to his feet. "A man of my power, my status, doesn't have to. You don't get it, Mr. Stuart. Men like me will always get what they want, and right now, I want Miss Kelly." He spun on his heels and pointed at Ben. "Men like you will end up buried in a forsaken place like this. No progress, no vision of what the world will become. Our mutual friend, Miss Kelly, seems unable to understand this, either."

"Oh, she understood you perfectly." Ben looked around at the half dozen men Irving had assembled. Someone had placed a bandage over the wound, but blood seeped through. "She believes you're weak, and she's right. How else do you explain all of these men just to get me to . . . do what exactly, *Mr.* Irving? Haven't you figured out yet? You can't win. Kill me, and they'll come after you. Don't, and they still will. If they don't, I know of a certain bank in Rapid City eager to see you behind bars."

Irving cleared his throat and chanced a quick glance at his men. "You know nothing."

"I know you can't pay these men what you've promised." Ben enjoyed watching Irving fidget. "I know you won't ever get Amanda's land you want to steal from her or the gold."

"Quiet!" Irving stepped close—too close for his own safety. Ben considered his options. His head ached worse than the time he'd been thrown off a mustang that had a disagreement with a saddle, and he knew it wouldn't be long before he lost too much blood to find his way of out this mess.

"Answer a question for me. If you are planning to kill me, I deserve the courtesy."

Irving stepped back and waved his hand. "Why not?"

"Why take me? It won't benefit you, so why do it? Is it because one of your men failed to kill her?"

Irving shot a quick look to one of the men standing to Ben's right. Good, now Ben knew who pulled the trigger that nearly ended Amanda's life. "Are you the one who attacked Jake? Knives seem to be your weapon of choice." Ben held up his bloody hand—his blood. "Is this your handy work?"

Irving brushed away dust only he could see from his wool coat. "It doesn't matter why you're here when you won't be around to see the results."

"Why don't you tell your men what fate awaits you back in Dakota? Let them decide if what they're about to do is worth going to prison for."

One of the six men—not the one who shot Amanda—spoke up. "What's he sayin,' Mr. Irving?"

"Nothing!" Irving smoothed the front of his shirt. "It's nothing."

"But what does he mean we ain't gonna get paid?"

Another man stepped forward. "Yeah, Mr. Irving. What's he talkin' about?"

"You're going to believe this fool? Have I not promised you more money than you can earn in a lifetime?"

The men nodded. Only one, the one Ben wanted most, didn't appear to care. His demeanor conveyed a man who killed for either the enjoyment or the money. Either way, he seemed indifferent, perhaps even amused.

Ben chanced a step forward. Irving held

up his hands when a few of the men advanced. "Now, don't worry. Mr. Stuart knows it's fruitless to try and escape." Irving motioned to one of his men. "Give me your gun, Stutz."

Stutz reluctantly handed his gun over. No sooner did Irving grip the handle then he cocked the lever and pulled the trigger. Stutz crumbled, face first, to the ground. Irving smiled and pointed the gun at Ben. "It's time you and I came to an understanding."

RAMSEY RODE HARD AND fast, arriving at the ranch with a lathered horse. He hopped off the sable gelding before it came to a full stop. Colton had brought a wagon to the house so he could drive Elizabeth and Amanda into town. Colton patted one of the horse's backs and faced Ramsey. "We didn't expect you back so soon."

"Neither did I." Ramsey, out of breath, turned when a young man he didn't recognize approached, his long legs ambling between a run and skip. "Who is this?"

"Levi Gibbs, new kid Ben hired." Colton took the reins from Ramsey's hand and passed them to Levi. "Look after his horse, and if you see Ethan out there, tell him we need him at the house."

"Yes, sir." Levi strolled back to the barn, talking to the tired horse as he went.

"What's going on, Ramsey?" Colton asked when Levi was far enough away not to overhear.

"Irving is on his way here, if he isn't already, I'm sure of it."

"Ethan told us about Cobb's telegram."

Ramsey stilled. "If you got a telegram, it wasn't from Cobb. He's in Briarwood at Doc Brody's. He caught a bullet in Bozeman when he stepped into the middle of a gun fight between a deputy and a drunk. He didn't want to wait any more than I did, so I patched him up and now the doc is seeing to him. What else did the telegram say?"

"That Cobb stayed behind to finish some business. A few of us were surprised but figured you knew what you were doing."

"I would have left him behind, but there was no need. Cobb has proven to be more trustworthy than I expected, even stepped in front of a bullet when it could have been me. The telegram had to have come from one of Irving's men. Trying to throw us off his trail, give Irving more time?"

Colton nodded. "And we believed it."

"You had no reason not to," Ramsey said.

Ethan approached at a run. "What's going on, Ramsey?"

"Where's Gabriel?"

"He went to find Ben. How'd you get back so fast?"

Ramsey relayed everything he'd just told Colton. Ethan didn't speak until after

Ramsey finished. "You're sure Irving is here now?"

Ramsey nodded. "I'd bet on it. He wasn't in Iron City when we arrived, and everyone we spoke with hadn't seen him in over a week. He was probably on his way here even before Cobb and I showed up in Iron City. If he took the train through to Bozeman and rode up from there, he's probably here. Wasted trip if it hadn't been for Deputy Isaac Porter."

AMANDA LISTENED FROM INSIDE the library where she'd been reading while Brenna worked on her needlepoint. The cool spring breeze drifted through the open window, along with their voices. She set the book down and left the library in a rush, Brenna's concerned voice asking what was wrong. When she stepped onto the front porch, the men fell silent. "Did I hear you, right? Baldwin Irving might be here in Briarwood?"

Ethan walked up the steps of the porch. "He might be. Gabe rode out to get Ben. When he gets here, we'll start a search. If Irving is in the area, someone in town or on one of the neighboring farms might have seen something."

Amanda gripped the railing and looked at Ramsey. "What did you mean about Isaac Porter?"

"He told me he helped you escape that night from Iron City to save your life."

"True."

Ramsey shook his head and stepped closer. "He also said to watch out for Irving, said he's not as afraid to get his hands dirty as we might have thought."

Amanda held a hand to her chest, searching for the locket she kept close to her heart, the one her mother had given her as a child. Holding it somehow made her feel closer to her parents, gave her strength she might not otherwise have had. "Gabriel hasn't come back with Ben yet. Do you think . . ." She noticed the exchange of looks between the men. "What is it?"

Ethan placed a hand on Amanda's shoulder and looked toward the door when his wife stepped outside. "Go back inside with Brenna. I promise one way or another, we'll settle this. You will be safe again, Amanda."

"What about everyone else?" She looked from face to face waiting for someone to offer her a solution which didn't involve harm coming to any of them.

Colton semi-smiled and said, "We've been in worse scrapes."

"What is it about Irving that is so unusual, Ramsey? You said—"

"I know what I said." Ramsey removed his hat and spared a glance at Ethan. "Irving's dangerous, if what Deputy Porter told us is to be believed. He's not the weak man who stands behind his men. Before he became the banker you and everyone else knew him as, he robbed, murdered, and had no qualms about destroying families."

"How could Deputy Porter know all this? And why would the bank hire—"

"Porter knew Irving before he became Baldwin Irving. Said he went by the name of William Irving. Baldwin was his father's name."

Ethan said, "We're ending this, before he has a chance to—"

"He wants me." Amanda stared hard at Ethan. "I can give him what he wants."

"No!" Brenna stepped forward and gripped Amanda's arm. "That's not an option."

Amanda covered Brenna's hand and silently pleaded with her to understand. To them all, she said, "The original plan was to draw out Irving. He's here, and the only way to be certain he's either caught or . . . can't come back, is to trade me. I have only to sign over the land."

Objections sounded from all around, except from Ramsey. "We can guarantee her safety."

"No you can't." Brenna walked down the steps, hands on hips, and faced down her brother. "You know how much I love and trust all of you, but it's not possible to guarantee that once this Irving has her, she'll be safe. Besides, am I the only one who believes this is about more than the land? If that's all he wanted, as Amanda has said before, there are easier ways." Brenna pleaded with them all. "This feels wrong, as though this man is setting a trap for Amanda. Except we don't know why."

"The marshals have been informed of our suspicion and the possibility that Irving is here," Ethan began, "but the last time we waited for the law to catch up, we almost lost Eliza. That's not going to happen again."

HE'S MAD, BEN THOUGHT, and watched Irving step over the man he had just killed. He ordered the others to drag Stutz's body deeper into the woods and to leave him for the wild animals. It was evident they had been wrong about Irving, even when all of the evidence pointed to a citified dandy, desperate and weak.

"You should have stayed away from her, Mr. Stuart." Irving pressed the gun into Ben's wounded side. "I kept waiting for her to return, and I hoped she was killed somewhere between Dakota and Montana. I shouldn't have trusted Cobb. I saw it in his eyes when he found out I'd burned the store to the ground."

Ben gritted his teeth against the pain and released a steady breath when Irving removed the gun's barrel. "You had someone follow Cobb, didn't you? That's how you figured out where she was, how you got here so soon."

"Very good, Mr. Stuart." Irving made a

show of wiping Ben's blood from the tip of the gun barrel. "When we saw the fellow take her from town, my man stood down. How much easier if she was killed by someone else. Of course, you ruined it."

"It's just money, Irving."

Irving rushed forward and shoved the gun under Ben's chin, not a difficult feat since Ben stood several inches taller. All he had to do was pull the gun from Irving's grasp. He didn't worry about the others—except for the one who shot Amanda, who had attempted to kill Jake. Ben saw in the man's expression that he wouldn't hesitate to kill Ben.

"It's just money? Just money!" A maniacal laugh escaped Irving's lips as he swung the pistol around in the air. "Oh, it's so much more." He lowered his voice to a whisper and stepped closer so the others couldn't hear. "You see, Mr. Stuart, I'll be the greatest gold baron in the west once I'm finished. The gold will all be mine.

You, those high and mighty Gallaghers, and the insipid bankers, will all know what it is to bow to me." He eased back a few inches, let loose another round of raucous laughter before he tossed the gun to the only man who appeared like he wanted to use it.

"Gentlemen. Make Mr. Stuart comfortable. We want him alive for Miss Kelly's funeral."

31

FLANKED BY ETHAN AND Colton with Ramsey riding in front, they approached his and Eliza's spacious cabin. Amanda recognized Gabriel's horse but not the one without a saddle. Ramsey shouted as they got closer, a collective relief settling over the small group when they heard Eliza call back.

A few seconds later, both Eliza and Gabriel stepped outside, Gabriel pressing a cloth to the back of his head.

Ramsey dismounted and pulled his wife aside and spoke with her quietly. Amanda didn't know what they'd said to each other, but the exchange was one she recognized—concern, aggravation, trust, and an abundance of love. She'd witnessed it plenty during her time at Hawk's Peak and not just between Ramsey and Eliza.

"What happened, Gabe?" Ethan asked.

"Someone got me from behind. He was waiting inside when I rode up. I noticed the smoke from the chimney and thought Eliza might be home." Gabriel lowered the cloth, now stained red in the center. "I'll live, but Eliza found Ben's horse tangled up in some bushes east of here."

Amanda remained on her horse and looked at Eliza. "Are you sure it was Ben's?"

"I'm sure." She nodded toward her husband. "Gabe and I were about to ride out and look for him. Ben is a superb horseman, and it's not likely he was thrown."

"Gabe should go back to the house and to Isabelle."

"Not this time," Gabriel said. "We have

a deal, and this time it's me and Eliza." Ethan and Gabriel seemed to stare one another down, and Eliza had the gall to smirk before she mounted the painted horse with no saddle.

Amanda had heard about this "deal" once from Brenna. They'd agreed years ago that Hawk's Peak would never be without a Gallagher. If something happened to two of them, there would still be one to ensure the ranch and the legacy their parents built would live on. Brenna had said it more to her son, Jacob, but Amanda had been in the room while they enjoyed afternoon tea. Even though a new generation of Gallaghers had been born, Ethan apparently planned to hold the siblings to their agreement.

After a minute, Gabriel nodded once and moved toward his horse. He didn't need help up, but he closed his eyes— perhaps against pain or dizziness—once he was in the saddle.

Eliza asked, "Is this the work of one of Irving's hired men?"

"We don't know yet, of course." Ramsey remounted his gelding and told Gabriel and Eliza a shortened version of what he'd told the others. "We don't have a lot of time."

"And Amanda is here because . . ." Eliza began, and then turned incredulous. "You can't be thinking to use her as bait. I know that was your idea," she said to Amanda, "but it's crazy."

"Calm down, sweetheart." Ramsey tweaked her nose. "I have that all worked out, and your brother agrees with me."

"That's because he's as loco as you are."

Colton said, "Eliza, if you want to tell me where you found the horse, we'll track them from there."

Eliza exhaled and gave Amanda a quick study. "I sure hope you know what you're doing."

Amanda tightened the reins in her fist.

"So do I."

THE BLEEDING STOPPED ONCE, but every time Ben moved, he felt it seep again from the wound. His head still throbbed, and he knew he'd already lost a lot of blood. They didn't stand down, not once, though one of the doubters glanced in his direction every few minutes.

He'd tried to turn the men against Irving, but it seemed they were more interested in possibly getting whatever money the banker promised them. Ben couldn't make such a promise. Once he found a way out of this mess, he intended to see every one of them ended up behind bars or in the ground. At this point, he wasn't picky about which.

"Eli, bring him over here."

Eli. Now he knew his name. The man who shot Amanda gave Irving a scalding look before he shoved the tip of his pistol against Ben's back. "You gonna do exactly as I say, you hear?"

Ben held his hands out to the side. "I hear you."

Irving gesticulated with his hands and stepped close to Ben. "You might not be as important to Miss Kelly as I presumed. No one has come for you. Why? We left that horse of yours where they'd find him."

"You've overplayed your hand, Irving. The others at the ranch won't let her come, and while they have a reputation for taking care of family, I'm just a ranch foreman. They're smart enough to know this is a trap, and they aren't going to risk the safety of either Amanda or their other men."

Irving tapped a finger against his pursed lips. "They'll just let you die?" His loud, grating laughter filled the air once more. "I think you're lying to me, Mr. Stuart. Do you know what I do to liars?" He leaned in close. "Why don't we ask Miss Kelly, hmmm?"

Ben didn't know what Irving meant, unless he spoke of Amanda's father. "I really don't care."

"You know, Mr. Stuart, if I didn't dislike you so much, you'd make a good employee. Not too smart, though." Irving tapped the side of his head. "Only a fool would think he could outwit me and live to tell about it."

"Rider coming in!" Another man emerged from the trees, someone Ben hadn't seen before now. He figured they'd had a lookout, and he'd guess this newcomer, who couldn't be more than eighteen, was the last of Irving's men. "It's a woman, Mr. Irving."

"Is she alone?"

"No, sir. Ridin' in slow and calm like with Sheriff Cobb. I done made sure of it, sir." The young man looked around. "Where's my brother?"

Was Stutz the man's brother? Ben wondered. He didn't see how the banker would talk his way of this one, and he doubted Irving cared.

"He's lookout on the other side of the clearing, beyond the trees," Eli answered before he spit on the ground near Ben's feet. "Don't want no one sneaking up on us, now do we?"

"No, sir," the boy said. "Should I go back to lookout, Mr. Irving?"

"You do that, boy." When the kid turned his back and walked away, Irving nodded to Eli. Ben realized what they intended before Eli withdrew the long, silver blade from the sheath at his side. He lunged for the boy, but Ben got to him first.

SHE DIDN'T HAVE ELIZA'S skills with a horse or gun—almost no skills if she was going to be honest with herself—but Amanda could have used them to bolster her confidence.

The mare she rode didn't seem to need special instructions. Amanda held the reins and guided her toward the trees, just as Ramsey had instructed. What she didn't expect was for anyone to join her.

Hooves on the ground was a sound to which she'd become accustomed to, but she didn't foresee the arrival of Stratton Cobb. His arm wrapped close to his chest in a thick, white bandage, his face pale and in need of a shave, he winced when he drew his horse back to walk alongside hers.

"What are you doing here?" She looked all around for some sign the others were aware of Cobb's arrival. Of course they would have seen him, and for whatever reason, chose to let him join her.

"Hell if I know."

"I don't trust you or like you, Mr. Cobb, and I don't want you here."

He had the audacity to smile. "I don't much like you either, Miss Warren. See, I remembered the right name this time."

They would soon be at the edge of the

woods. She told herself to trust the others, though she didn't know where they were hiding. "How did you know I'd be here?"

"You didn't think they'd let you ride in there alone, did you?"

Her mare twisted its head to nip at the other horse when it got too close. "How did you know? You've been laid up at the doctor's clinic."

"It was Ramsey's idea. Of course, the doctor gave me something and knocked me out. When I came to and saw he'd stitched me up, I rode out to the ranch. A pretty woman with a Scottish accent pointed a rifle at me. Gabriel Gallagher joined her, which is good because I think she was ready to put a few holes in my hide."

"Gabriel told you where we'd gone?"

"It seems he was expecting me." Cobb ignored her mare's annoyance and drew his horse close to hers. "This will go better for you and your friend if they think you hate me."

"That should be easy."

He reached for her reins and pulled them from her grasp. Amanda reached for them only to find a pistol pointed at her. "You're not hurt then? Ramsey said—"

"It hurts like hell. Now, do me a favor and act scared."

"What makes you think I'm not?"

Cobb didn't answer her. His injured shoulder was unbound, and Amanda caught the grimace. She said nothing else as they disappeared into the shadows of the trees. One hundred feet inside the forest, they stopped. Amanda smelled smoke from a campfire, and a few seconds later, men emerged from the trees, six in total, including Baldwin Irving.

Her heartbeat escalated when she didn't see Ben among them.

"Keep quiet and you might live through this," Cobb whispered and continued to hold the reins to her horse. He dismounted first, with some difficulty. To her surprise, he didn't instruct her to get down.

"I knew you wouldn't let me down, Cobb." Irving patted him on his wounded shoulder, forcing Cobb to nod instead of respond.

"The Gallaghers aren't too bright. People will always believe you when you tell them what they want to hear."

"Right you are!" Irving circled the front of the mare and sneered at Amanda. "You gave me quite the chase, Miss Kelly . . . ah, yes, it's Miss Warren now. You see, I always achieve what I set out to do. We could have solved our little problem back in Iron City if you would have cooperated."

"You burned down my father's store and put me in jail. If it hadn't been for—"

"Deputy Porter? Yes, what a disappointment he turned out to be. Unfortunately, I learned of his weaknesses too late. No matter, he won't live long after we return. You, on the other hand, are not going to be so lucky."

Amanda looked around once more at the men's faces. "Where is he?"

"You mean Mr. Stuart?" Irving motioned to two of the men who ran farther into the trees. "He killed my best gun. I had no choice."

The men dragged another by his arms into the small clearing. A gasp escaped Amanda's lips, and before she gave consideration to her actions, she slid off the horse and ran toward Ben. They'd dropped him on the ground. He was too big to turn over on her own. "What have you done?"

Irving linked his hands behind his back and walked toward Amanda and Ben. He appeared to enjoy towering over her, and after a few seconds, he hunched down. "He served his purpose. Now, my dear. I have a document here I'd like you to sign. Once you have, my men will tie you up, giving us a chance to ride away, and eventually someone will come looking for you."

Infused with anger and disgust, Amanda said, "Then why try to kill me?"

"Now, my dear. If I wanted you dead, you would be."

Confused, Amanda stared into Irving's stony eyes. "I don't understand. I nearly died from that gunshot!"

"Yes, Eli does enjoy his work a bit too much." Irving rose, all traces of amusement fleeing his expression. "If you'd done what I asked the first time, none of this senseless violence would have been necessary."

"Done what you—you're mad!"

Irving shrugged and removed a folded sheet of paper from his inside coat pocket. "Now, sign this, and we'll be done."

Amanda accepted the document and quickly scanned the few paragraphs before tossing it at Irving's feet. "I'll never sign that."

"You will."

Before Amanda realized what was going to happen, two men moved forward and lifted Ben to his feet. She reached for Ben, only to be held back by someone in desperate need of a bath. "No! Can't you see, he needs a doctor. You're killing him!"

"What's going on, Irving?" Cobb stepped forward, the reins of both horses loose in his hands.

"If you had done your job, I never would have had to come to this miserable place!" Irving's shout carried through the trees, disturbing a flock of birds hiding among the branches. Their squalls and cries echoed above as they flew away. He flung a wrist toward Ben. "Stab him for every time she refuses."

Amanda experienced a wave of fear and studied Ben. How much longer did he have? His pallor and heavy breathing grew worse by the minute. She didn't . . . Did he move or was she hoping for a miracle? She watched him closely, ignoring Irving. Ben did move, and she prayed the others hadn't noticed. "I'll sign! Just don't hurt him anymore."

"Good girl."

Whoever held onto Amanda released her. She read the wrinkled document once more. "How am I to sign it?"

One of Irving's men produced a small board, and on top placed a dip pen and ink well. Amanda set the paper on the board, and with a shaky hand, raised the pen over the ink. She turned and faced Baldwin Irving.

She wanted to put a bullet from Ben's gun into the man's chest. Even when she believed herself safe and happy in Briarwood, a hole in her heart had remained filled with anger and enmity since the night her father was murdered. If she didn't stop now, how would she ever move forward? She lowered the pen. "You won't let us live. You were never going to let me live. I want to know why because this isn't just about the gold, is it?"

Irving looked momentarily surprised. Good. She didn't want him thinking too much right now. "Ramsey, whom I'm sure you'll meet soon, told me that money, love, and hate are the most powerful motivators for evil, but there are easier ways to get money."

"Amanda, don't say anything else."

She shook her head at Cobb, mustered every bit of strength she could, and turned her attention back to Irving. She hoped he couldn't see her body shake, and she didn't know how she kept her voice steady. "Is it love or hate, Mr. Irving?"

"You don't know what you're talking about." He spat the words and handed her the pen. "Now sign."

"I suspect you want the gold, but you meant for me to die that night in the store along with my father, didn't you?"

Amanda couldn't prevent the moisture from forming in her eyes and did her best to keep tears from falling. "Your plan didn't work, but if you're going to kill us anyway, I want to know why."

Irving stared at her for a long time before heaving a sigh. "You're right, I am going to kill you, and Mr. Stuart, but first you'll still sign this deed."

"Tell me why you've done all this, Mr. Irving. I deserve to know since you're going to put a bullet in both of us."

Irving became . . . dark. Amanda could think of no other way to describe the sudden change. "Your worthless father didn't deserve what he had. I could have been everything to your mother, and then to you—given you everything!"

"What are you talking about? I never—"

"You aren't going to die right away, Amanda Warren. First, I'm going to have what you denied me all those years, and then your friend here," Irving kicked Ben in the side, "is going to watch you die by my hand."

The significance of what Irving meant crushed Amanda's already wavering calm. Reed Slater had been dangerous, obsessed. She didn't have a word for what Irving had just confessed. She doubted he realized what he'd said. His dark and hollow eyes showed no sympathy, no mercy.

"I was never yours. My mother was never yours! All this time, everything you've done to us, is because of what you couldn't have?"

"And the gold, of course." Irving waved a hand, almost as if to dismiss her. He turned back and stood close enough for Amanda to feel his breath on her skin. From the corner of her vision, she noticed Cobb take a step forward. "We could have been rich together, the perfect affluent couple." He lowered his voice to a whisper.

"You should have been kinder to me, Amanda."

The palm of her hand connected with Irving's face, knocking him back a few inches. Seconds later, he returned the favor, only the force of his slap nearly sent her plunging backward.

"Your father was nothing, and now he has nothing! He lost wife because he was too weak of a man to give her what she needed. He lost his life, and now I'll kill the most precious thing to him before I take his land and gold. Even in the grave, he'll know he's nothing!"

32

BEN HAD HEARD ENOUGH. The madness behind Irving's true motives had been revealed. He didn't know why Cobb had ridden in with her—it was a confusing piece of the puzzle—and Ben realized he didn't have much time left before he passed out or died from loss of blood.

Amanda's cries, her shouts of anger and disbelief, tore at his heart. He wanted to push away from the men and protect her, assure her that nothing horrible would ever touch her life again, but he couldn't. Not yet, and certainly not in his condition.

Ben's only hope now was to trust Stratton Cobb. He raised his head, consuming more energy than he had to spare, and saw Amanda lunge toward Irving. Whatever stores of life he still possessed rose to the surface, and he threw himself away from his captors, giving him enough of an advantage to fight back.

The moment Ben moved, gunshots sounded. He reached for the pistol in the holster of the man closest to him and didn't hesitate to pull the trigger. When the yelling stopped, Ben saw three men on their knees, hands raised above their heads. Three men lay on the ground, dead. One shot by Ben, and the other two . . . he saw Cobb's gun drawn but the dead man fell too far away. He looked to the trees and saw Ethan and Ramsey emerge.

"Amanda!" He could barely move but managed to stumble to her. When he set a hand on her arm, she turned, and Irving crumbled at her feet. She held a bloody knife at her waist.

AMANDA BLOCKED OUT THE voices, the echo of the gunshots, and saw only Irving's wide, pale eyes. She watched disbelief cross his face over what she'd done, as though he couldn't believe she had the courage, the audacity to fight him, to take the knife he'd clearly meant to use on her.

Wouldn't a gun have been easier, quicker? Amanda thought. He could have avoided getting blood on his expensive clothes. Irving's expression said he couldn't believe the slip of a woman was able to grab the knife from him. Amanda sensed the moment in their struggle when he'd been distracted by the gunfire and lost focus. She watched as Irving released his final breath.

"Amanda?"

The knife rolled off her open hand to land beside Irving. "That's for my father, and for my freedom."

Ben wrapped her in his embrace, and

she immediately pulled away. Blood from his wound had transferred to her dress. "You're still losing a lot of blood, Ben. We have to get you to Doc Brody."

Ethan and Cobb hurried to either side of Ben to support him. Amanda noticed Ben's eyes were no longer open. Colton rode into the clearing, pulling two horses behind him. They helped Ben to Ethan's stallion, and Ethan swung up behind him. "I'll get him back to the ranch. Amanda, he'll want you there when he wakes up."

She managed to climb onto the horse after two tries and with a little boost from Cobb. Amanda met Cobb's gaze. "Thank you. I truly didn't believe you were on our side, but I'm grateful you are."

"We don't like each other, Miss Warren, there's no denying it. I don't expect you to trust me, either, but maybe someday."

"I don't understand you, Mr. Cobb."

He tipped the edge of his hat, and to her surprise and mild annoyance, he smiled.

"You don't need to."

Amanda looked at the four men on their knees. Ethan said to Ramsey, "We'll be back with a wagon for the bodies." He said to Cobb, "Are you willing to see this through?"

Cobb looked down at Irving's lifeless body and nodded.

They rode away from the grisly scene as quickly as Ethan could without Ben falling over. Colton soon gained distance on them, and all Amanda could do was pray he'd get the doctor back to the ranch on time. She had so many questions for Ethan, and every time she looked over to ask, her eyes fell on Ben. She couldn't lose him, not after all they'd been through.

"Is he going to live?"

Ethan didn't answer. He looked at her long and hard before he urged his stallion to go a little faster.

Their welcoming party at the house consisted of Catie and Andrew, joined soon after by two of the ranch hands who helped lift Ben off the horse. Ethan pointed to the house. "Please take him upstairs, to the right, last room at the end of the hallway."

Amanda wanted to follow them but knew they'd have to cut away his clothes and check his wounds. She needed to find Elizabeth who would, Amanda hoped, at least know how to keep Ben alive until the doctor arrived. Please, hurry Colton! Amanda tripped on the steps going up to the porch. Ethan caught her before she fell forward.

"He's going to be all right, Amanda."

She looked up at him. "We don't know that, but thank you for saying it."

"What happened to him?" Andrew's frightened voice reminded the adults they weren't alone.

"He had to fight off some pretty mean beasts," Ethan said and crouched down in front of Andrew, careful not to let the boy come too close to his stained clothes.

"Like wolves?"

"A little like wolves. What are you two doing outside?" Ethan stood and asked Catie, "Are Brenna and the baby napping? Come to think of it, why is it so quiet, and where's Gabriel?"

A scream rent the air contradicting Ethan's last statement.

"Ibby's having a baby!" Andrew grinned and leaned against the railing. "I get to be a big brother."

Amanda didn't stop to ask anything more. She hurried past Ethan, though he followed close behind. They halted at the base of the stairs when the sweet sound of a baby's cry filled the air. Exhaustion from her ordeal could not compare to the elation that came with the joyful sounds of new life. The tears fell in earnest, sobs wracking her body.

"I COULD GIVE UP my practice with as busy

as you folks keep me these days." Doc Brody cleaned his hands in the porcelain bowl filled with water and accepted the cloth Amanda handed him.

"Promise me he'll be okay, doctor."

Doc Brody latched his black, leather medical bag and faced Amanda, his face grim. "It's too soon to say, Miss Warren. Elizabeth's nursing skills helped before I arrived, but he's lost a lot of blood. He's strong, though, so he has a fighting chance. Make sure he stays in bed for the rest of the week. He won't be able to get up, anyway. He'll need to take it easy for a couple of weeks while he heals." Turning to the group, the doctor asked, "Anyone care to tell me how Ben came to have four knife wounds and a bullet in his leg?"

When no one answered, the doctor sighed and walked to the bedroom door. "I'll return in a few days to check on the sutures. He'll need his bandages changed twice a day. When he wakes up, tell him to stay in bed or the next time I'll see him will be at his funeral."

The doctor gave each person in the room another stern look before he turned and walked down the hallway, Elizabeth accompanied him to show him out and express the family's gratitude.

Amanda didn't notice when everyone else except Brenna filed out of the room. She lowered her weary body into the chair next to the bed and watched Ben's chest rise and fall with each breath.

"You should sleep."

Amanda turned at the sound of Brenna's soft voice. "I can't yet. Perhaps later, when I know he'll come through."

"He's a strong one, our Ben."

"If you're going to tell me he's suffered worse—"

"Now don't put words in my mouth. Truth is, I don't know his story. Ethan's told me a bit, but I learned to look on Hawk's Peak as a place of refuge and the people on it as foundlings. We all arrive a tad heartbroken and running from ourselves or someone else. We heal here, we become better, stronger versions of who we're meant to be. It's a place where journeys end and new paths begin." Brenna embraced Amanda from behind. "He's lucky to have you, and you him." She slipped out of the room before Amanda could respond.

33

Two weeks later.

AMANDA GRIPPED THE NEW railing one of the men had added to the bridge over the stream. She tilted her head back, closed her eyes, and welcomed the pine-scented breeze sweeping over her skin while the sun caressed her face. The warm rays soaked through her clothes, and she let the edges of her shawl slip down her shoulders. Nature's song soothed her as no other music ever could. The clear water gurgled as it flowed and swished over rocks and pebbles.

She looked up when a pair of red-tailed hawks screeched above, their calls carried off by the wind as they circled and swooped. She imagined a poor creature hiding on the ground below and hoped it might be spared. The dancing pair soon flew to a nearby tree free of foliage and settled on a thick branch.

"Pretty day."

Her lips curved into a smile before she turned around. "You should still be resting."

"I won't tell if you won't." Ben ambled to the bridge and sat on one of the railings. "I escaped. If Elizabeth had her way, I'd be in bed for another month."

"I agree with her."

The dark circles under his eyes now left only a faint shadow. He'd lost a few pounds during the first week in bed, though Elizabeth assured him she'd take care of that in no time at all. Her breath hitched when she remembered what the doctor had said about the number of wounds, and how Ben had been lucky. One of the knife lacerations landed only a few inches from his heart. To Amanda, he looked perfect.

"A few minutes won't hurt." She moved to stand beside him. "Have you seen Gabriel and Isabelle's baby yet?"

"August Gallagher." Ben chuckled and eased off his injured leg. "I'd say the family has ensured their legacy will live on."

"He's perfect, just like little Rebecca." Amanda brushed away a few errant tears.

"Hey, another Gallagher is a good thing. As far as I'm concerned, the world can't have too many."

"It's not that. These are happy tears. Ever since . . ."

"You've been to visit me every day during my recovery, and every time I bring up Irving and what happened, you change the subject. I think it's time you talk about it. If not with me, then maybe—"

"No." She pressed a finger to his lips and dropped her hand. "I had to come to terms with killing Irving before I could talk about it." Amanda slipped her hand into Ben's, drawing on his warmth. "I imagined what I would do if given the chance to find justice for my father. It wasn't all about the gold. Irving hated my father all because the women who loved Fergus Kelly didn't give a second thought to Baldwin Irving. He truly was out of his mind. If I hadn't taken the knife, he would have killed me."

"Love and hate are close friends. Sometimes it's difficult to tell them apart." Ben cupped her face with one of his strong hands. "What that man thought he felt wasn't love, Amanda, it was possession. You know what love is, you knew it all your life because of your parents' devotion to each other and to you. Knowing love and being loved was never a question in your life."

"And you, Ben, did you ever know love?"

"My mother. She wasn't strong, and she made some mistakes, but I felt her love. I carried a lot of hate with me for a long time, and I didn't know if I'd ever let myself have what Ethan and Gabriel and Eliza found. I watched them all, and I wondered if there was more for me . . . until you." His smile reached his warm, brown eyes. "Brenna recently told me that Hawk's Peak is a place where journeys end and new paths begin."

Amanda's laughter bubbled up and rang loud. When she settled back down, she said, "Our dear Brenna. She told me the same thing after the doctor bandaged you up. He couldn't promise me you would live and a part of me wished I had the opportunity to kill Irving all over again."

"Ethan told me your other news, about the land in Iron City."

Amanda had given a great deal of thought to the information—and offer— Ethan had relayed to her. "Irving's partner in the mine had only visited the mine and Iron City once, leaving the operation to be managed by Irving. When he was contacted about Irving's death, he sent a telegram. It seems Irving mentioned his plans to buy my land, and the partner, a Mr. Sykes, made a new offer—a generous one. He promised to leave one acre where my parents are buried, untouched and preserved."

"Have you signed the papers yet?"

"It's one of the reasons why I'm out here, thinking." She leaned against the railing and smiled up at Ben. "I'm going to sign, and Mr. Sykes also promised to replace the general store and see to it the people of Iron City are taken care of. I don't know what I'll do with all the money, but I know I'd like to see it used for good."

"And you won't have any regrets about not going back?"

"I'll visit my mother and father, but in truth, they've never left me. They'll remain on the land they both loved, but this is where I belong. My greatest sorrow is they didn't have the opportunity to meet you. They would have loved you. And this place. I wish—"

"There's too much in this world we can't control, no guarantees, and always the chance of losing those who matter most. No matter where I am, or if one of us leaves this earth before the other, you'll never lose me."

The last ache of pain and hate around her heart dissolved.

She stepped into his arms, felt his heart beat in time with hers. Ben kissed her. Not a frenzied kiss of passion but rather one of hope that told her they had all the time they needed to be together.

He leaned his forehead against hers. "If you're willing to finish the journey with me, I can give you one more guarantee." Ben held her hand to his heart. "You'll never have to wonder if you're loved. No matter what, you'll always know."

"No matter what." Amanda pressed her lips to his once more, leaned deeper into his embrace, and together they gazed over the land. They'd traveled their own perilous roads but found the way to Hawk's Peak. Amanda believed it was her mother and father's spirits who had guided her home.

THE END

Thank you for reading *Journey to Hawk's Peak*!

From the author . . .

Amanda and Ben's journey was somewhat bittersweet because there was always the chance this would be the end, but it didn't take long for me to realize I couldn't say goodbye. I don't know when or how often they'll return, but you haven't heard the last from the Gallaghers of Hawk's Peak or the people of Briarwood, Montana.

Interested in reading more by MK McClintock? Try her British Agent novels—stories of romance, adventure, and mystery set in Victorian England. Available in print, large print, and e-book.

The Historical Romantic Mystery British Agent novels:
Book One – *Alaina Claiborne*
Book Two – *Blackwood Crossing*
Book Three – *Clayton's Honor*

Also try *A Home for Christmas: Short Story Collection*. A collection of three historical western short stories to inspire love and warm the heart, no matter the season. Available in print, large print, and e-book.

You may find all these and more at www.mkmcclintock.com.

Enjoy contemporary romance? MK also writes contemporary romantic thrillers, mysteries, and sweet contemporary romance as McKenna Grey.

Don't miss out on future books and special offers. Sign up for MK's periodic newsletter at www.mkmcclintock.com/newsletter.

MEET THE AUTHOR

MK McClintock is an award-winning author who has written several books and short stories, including the popular "Montana Gallagher" series, the "Crooked Creek" series set in post-Civil War Montana, and the highly-acclaimed "British Agent" novels. She spins tales of romance, adventure, and mystery set in bygone times. MK lives a quiet life in the Rocky Mountains.

Learn more about MK by visiting her website at www.mkmcclintock.com.

51333909R00253

Made in the USA
San Bernardino, CA
20 July 2017